At David C Cook, we equip the local church around
the corner and around the globe to make disciples.
Come see how we are working together—go to
www.davidccook.com. Thank you!

DAVID **C** COOK™

transforming lives together

HeartShaper BIBLE Storybook

HeartShaper
BIBLE
Storybook

Bible Stories to Fill Young Hearts with God's Word

Catherine DeVries

Illustrated by Laura Logan

DAVID C COOK

transforming lives together

HEARTSHAPER BIBLE STORYBOOK
Published by David C Cook
4050 Lee Vance Drive
Colorado Springs, CO 80918 U.S.A.

David C Cook U.K., Kingsway Communications
Eastbourne, East Sussex BN23 6NT, England

The graphic circle C logo is a registered trademark of David C Cook.

All rights reserved. Except for brief excerpts for review purposes,
no part of this book may be reproduced or used in any form
without written permission from the publisher.

Unless otherwise noted, all Scripture quotations are taken from the ESV®
Bible (The Holy Bible, English Standard Version®), copyright © 2001
by Crossway, a publishing ministry of Good News Publishers. Used by
permission. All rights reserved. Scripture quotations marked NASB are
taken from the New American Standard Bible®, copyright © 1960, 1995 by
The Lockman Foundation. Used by permission. (www.Lockman.org); NIV
are taken from the Holy Bible, NEW INTERNATIONAL VERSION®,
NIV®. Copyright © 1973, 2011 by Biblica, Inc.® Used by permission. All
rights reserved worldwide. NEW INTERNATIONAL VERSION® and
NIV® are registered trademarks of Biblica, Inc. Use of either trademark for
the offering of goods or services requires the prior written consent of Biblica,
Inc.; NLT are taken from the *Holy Bible*, New Living Translation, copyright
© 1996, 2007 by Tyndale House Foundation. Used by permission of Tyndale
House Publishers, Inc., Carol Stream, Illinois 60188. All rights reserved.

LCCN 2017963034
ISBN 978-0-7814-1273-5

© 2018 David C Cook

The Team: Catherine DeVries, Lindsay Black, Helen Macdonald,
Ed Stucky, Stephanie Bennett, Abby DeBenedittis, Susan Murdock
Cover Design: Amy Konyndyk
Illustrations: Laura Logan

Printed in China
First Edition 2018

1 2 3 4 5 6 7 8 9 10

011518

Contents

Note to Parents

Dear Parents,

This Bible storybook is meant to come alongside you and your child as you explore God's story together. Along the way you will meet children and families who are also exploring God's story together.

Each story opens and closes with a snapshot from a family's life that helps to frame the point of the Bible story. At the end of each story, you will see a question for you and your child. Feel free to ask your own questions as well, and take as long as you'd like talking together about your own experiences and thoughts about the story. This will help you connect the point of the story to your own lives.

Sometimes it may be easier to talk about points of the Bible story through the other families in the storybook, especially if your child hasn't experienced some things that are discussed, such as a death in the family, living in a big city, riding a school bus, working on a farm, or swimming at the beach.

In these stories, you'll meet Emma. She's an only child who lives with her mom in a suburb in the Pacific Northwest. Her father died during a tour overseas in the military. Emma and her mom enjoy hanging around the house and baking cookies together.

You'll also meet Jackson, who spends as much time as possible on his grandparents' farm in rural Pennsylvania. Jackson loves all things involving nature, animals, and the outdoors. Their life is simple but very deep and meaningful.

In the stories, you'll also get to know Olivia and Jacob. They are twins, and at times it's like they can read each other's minds. Jacob loves imagining himself fighting battles, being in charge, and making jokes, while Olivia is inquisitive and slower to speak but knows how to hold her own. They live on the west coast and spend a lot of family time on the beach.

The other child you'll meet is Bailey. She lives in a big city and often plays in a park with her older cousin Kira and her friends from school. Bailey loves sports and exploring the city. She thinks on her feet, and she is very brave.

At the end of each Bible story is a memory verse both of you can learn so you are storing up God's Word in your hearts together. Have fun learning together—wherever you go!

There are fifty-two stories in all, so you could consider reading one per week for a year's worth of devotional time together. Or just read it through as your family time allows.

May the Lord bless your conversations!

Our Creator Makes Us

Genesis 1–2

"Welcome to the botanical gardens, children. We're glad you're here! Have fun looking at all the plants. You'll find delicate flowers and strong, sturdy trees and all sorts of different colors. Go explore!"

"Jacob, come look! This flower is as big as my head!"

"Whoa. That's amazing. You know, this place reminds me of what I imagined the garden of Eden to look like, where Adam and Eve lived."

"Me too!"

LET'S LEARN FROM GOD'S WORD

In the beginning, God created. The very first thing God did was make something—something beautiful and complicated and perfect: our world.

God made stars that shine in galaxies thousands of light-years away. He made rivers that cut through mountains and snow that melts in the spring. He made caribou that run through the tundra and snakes that slither through the wetlands. He made colorful parrots and slow, slow turtles. And all of it, God said, was good.

Then God made people. A man and a woman named Adam and Eve. God said they were *very* good. They lived in a beautiful place called the garden of Eden. They were so happy to be with God! He walked with them in the shade, just before bedtime. They were good friends.

Many years later, God made you, and He said, "This is very good!" He is so happy when He looks at you. Did you know He sings songs over you too?

God wants you to enjoy Him and show His glory to the world. The whole world. But you can only do that if you know Him. So read on, because the more you learn about the Bible, the more you learn about who God is. And how very, very much He loves you.

"All right, kids, time to head back to school. What did you think of the botanical gardens? Pretty awesome, right?"

"*Psst.* Hey, Olivia! Check out my paper airplane. It's the garden of Eden."

"I love it! My favorite animal is the giraffe. God's so creative!"

HIDING GOD'S WORD IN YOUR HEART

What's your favorite part of God's creation?

The heavens declare the glory of God,
  and the sky above proclaims his handiwork. (Psalm 19:1)

Adam and Eve Have to Leave the Garden

Genesis 3

"Olivia, where'd you get that sparkly pencil? It's so cool."

"Thanks, Jacob! I'm borrowing it from a friend. She left it on her desk, so I thought she probably wasn't using it anymore. I'll give it back after I use it."

"I really like the eraser. It's awesome."

"Yeah, maybe we could just keep it. Would that be a big deal?

"Well, if she wasn't using it, it's probably okay. Right? It seems like you like it a lot more than she did."

"Yeah, I think I do too. Let's keep this a secret, okay?"

LET'S LEARN FROM GOD'S WORD

Someone else was in the garden of Eden with Adam and Eve: a snake. Well, it was really Satan, God's enemy. But he disguised himself as a tricky snake. He had one goal: to make Adam and Eve forget they were supposed to enjoy God and bring Him glory. That wasn't very nice, was it?

One day Eve was walking through the garden, probably smelling the flowers and playing with the animals, when that nasty snake made his move to make Eve forget about God's words. You see, God had told Adam and Eve they could eat from every tree in the garden except for one. But the snake told

Eve, "Sure, God told you not to eat this fruit. But is it a big deal? If you want it, you should take it."

Eve thought the fruit from that tree looked really yummy. She ate the fruit. Adam ate the fruit too. Then he blamed Eve, and she blamed the snake, and it turned into a huge mess.

God was sad. His people whom He loved had disobeyed Him. And sin always has consequences. Adam and Eve had to leave the garden. They had to find a new home and get clothes. They couldn't walk with God face-to-face anymore. Sin would now be a wall between people and God forever.

Well, not quite forever. God had a plan. One day He would send a Savior who would take away our sins. Then we would be right with God again.

"Olivia, did you win something at school today?"

"No, Mom. Why?"

"Well, where did you get that new pencil?"

"I just ... I thought I'd, eh, borrow it from my friend. But ... she didn't know I was borrowing it. I'm really, really sorry. I took what wasn't mine to take. I'll give it back to her tomorrow."

"I think that's a good choice, Olivia. It sounds like you learned a little bit from Adam and Eve's story?"

"Yes, I did."

HIDING GOD'S WORD IN YOUR HEART

What did you learn about sin from Adam and Eve's story?

God is faithful, and he will not let you be tempted beyond your ability.
(1 Corinthians 10:13)

Noah and the Great Flood

Genesis 6–8

"Why, Jackson! You certainly have a way with the horses. You're grooming them just like the pros down at the horse farms do. I'm impressed."

"Thanks, Grandpa. They're so gentle, even though they're big and strong."

"I think you should consider being a veterinarian when you grow up."

"A veter-a-what?"

"Ha-ha. That's a big word, isn't it? It means an animal doctor."

"Oh yes, I love animals. I'd love to do that job."

LET'S LEARN FROM GOD'S WORD

God had made an incredible world, but after a while, the people forgot they were supposed to glorify Him. Instead of putting God first and worshipping Him, they did whatever they wanted. They were selfish and mean.

God was angry that the people were hurting the earth and one another, so He decided to start over fresh with a family that loved Him. He chose Noah's family.

God told Noah it was going to rain. He gave Noah plans to build a really big boat called an ark. Just before the rain started, animals came to Noah from all over the earth. One male and one female of every type of animal—dogs, cats, elephants, tigers, porcupines, and even rats—walked into the ark.

Well, the rain came down and it didn't stop. It rained for forty whole days. That's more than a month. The whole earth—even the mountaintops—were covered with water. All the evil people died, but Noah and his family and the animals on the ark were safe because God protected them.

Finally, more than a year later, Noah and his family saw dry land. Do you know the first thing they did when they got out? They worshipped God. They thanked Him for saving them. They knew He was very serious about people putting Him first instead of spending their time sinning and pleasing only themselves.

"Jackson, these fresh eggs we get from the chickens each morning remind me of the fresh start that God gave people and the whole world after the Flood."

"What do you mean, Grandpa?"

"Well, these chickens give us tasty eggs that help us live strong, healthy lives every day. In the same way, God's faithfulness to us is new every morning. No matter what we've done the day before, we can wake up with a fresh start and put Him first each day."

HIDING GOD'S WORD IN YOUR HEART

♥

How will you put God first today?

The steadfast love of the LORD never ceases;
    his mercies never come to an end;
they are new every morning;
    great is your faithfulness. (Lamentations 3:22–23)

Abraham: A Huge Test

Genesis 12, 17, 22

"Mom, sometimes I wish we had a bigger family. I mean, I love that it's just me and you. But it would be fun to have a sister."

"I know, sweetie. I had hoped to have five or six kids. But God had different plans for us, didn't He? Daddy gave the ultimate sacrifice, and we miss him so much. But when I'm tempted to get frustrated with God, He reminds me of Abraham, and I remember to trust God because He knows what's best. He sees the big picture."

LET'S LEARN FROM GOD'S WORD

It was time for God to choose one man to be the father of His people, His chosen nation. This would be the family that Jesus—the One who would save us—would be born into. God's good news for all people would start with Abraham!

But Abraham and his wife, Sarah, had no children. How could a great nation come from them? God promised them that even though they were very old, they would become parents.

Abraham didn't understand, but he chose to believe. He knew it wasn't about what he could do but was about what God could do. So Abraham and Sarah moved to a new country and set themselves apart from everyone else to worship the one true God.

Abraham and Sarah had to wait a long time … years and years and years. But God's promise came true, and He gave them a baby boy—Isaac. They were so happy! They enjoyed many wonderful years together.

But then God talked with Abraham again and asked something they never imagined. God asked them to give Isaac back to Him. As before, Abraham was willing to obey. He knew God's plans were better than his own. So he took Isaac on a long walk up a steep hill, with a bundle of wood on his back. When they got to the top of the hill, Isaac looked around and asked his father where the sacrifice was. Abraham told him God would provide it. As Abraham was getting ready to give his precious son back to God, God said, "Stop!" He told Abraham to sacrifice a ram from the bushes instead.

Isaac grew up to be one of the fathers of God's chosen people. Jesus would one day be a part of that family too! And although God allowed Abraham to spare his son, God did not spare His own Son for us. He loves us so much!

"Mom, why would God ask Abraham to sacrifice Isaac?"

"That's a hard question, Emma, but I know this: God wanted to show Abraham that he could trust God. And the thing is, when a sacrifice for my sin was required, God didn't hold back His own Son. God allowed Jesus to die as the perfect sacrifice to take away the guilt of my sins and yours."

"Wow, Jesus died for our sins. I'm so thankful for His sacrifice."

HIDING GOD'S WORD IN YOUR HEART

♥

Why did Jesus die for us?

It was by faith that Abraham obeyed when God called him to leave home and go to another land that God would give him as his inheritance. He went without knowing where he was going.

(Hebrews 11:8 NLT)

Joseph: The Man Who Forgave His Brothers

Genesis 37–47

"Oof, ouch!"

"Oh, Bailey, are you okay? That looks like it really hurt."

"That was so mean! Darek, why did you kick me like that? You didn't even try to kick the ball. Ouch, my leg!"

"It wasn't my fault. You shouldn't have gotten in my way."

"Ugh, Kira, I'm really, really mad. I don't want to play with Darek anymore."

"Hang on, you guys. Let's talk about this. I know a story that might help."

LET'S LEARN FROM GOD'S WORD

Abraham's grandson Jacob had eleven sons. That's a lot of boys in one house! The boys fought a lot. And to make matters worse, their dad had a favorite. His name was Joseph.

Joseph's brothers knew Joseph was their dad's favorite son, and they hated him for it. They were so jealous it made them crazy. So crazy, in fact, that they sold him to slave traders headed to Egypt. They took Joseph's colorful coat he'd gotten as a gift from his dad, covered it in blood to make it look like he'd been killed, and then took it home to their dad. Can you imagine how sad their dad was?

Meanwhile, Joseph was lonely and scared. He was being taken to Egypt, a place he'd never been before. But God hadn't forgotten him.

When he got to Egypt, Joseph was sent to an important official of the king to work as a slave. He loved God, so he worked really hard and did a good job. Eventually, even though people lied about him and he had to spend time in jail, he became the king's most trusted adviser.

You want to know what's crazy? Joseph's brothers ended up in Egypt too. There was a famine back home, and they couldn't grow anything to eat. So they had to go to Egypt to ask for food. And you know who was in charge of giving out the food? That's right: Joseph.

It must have been tempting for Joseph to be mean to his brothers after what they had done to him. But remember, Joseph loved God. He knew that he hadn't been perfect in his life either, but God had forgiven him. So he forgave his brothers and gave them food. That forgiveness healed his family, and it's how God's people came to live in Egypt.

"If you guys don't forgive each other, you're not going to be able to let it go. So let's talk this out. Darek, what do you need to say to Bailey?"

"I'm sorry, Bailey. Are you okay?"

"Yes, Darek. I forgive you. And I'm sorry I said mean things when I was mad. But, Kira, could you get me some ice? It really hurts."

"Sure thing, Bailey. You're one tough kickball player."

HIDING GOD'S WORD IN YOUR HEART

Is there anyone you need to forgive today?

As the Lord has forgiven you, so you also must forgive.

(Colossians 3:13)

Moses: The Baby in the Basket

Exodus 2

"Mom, this is awesome. We're explorers going on an adventure to a never-before-discovered land."

"You're doing great, Emma. Oh, see those reeds over there? They'd be easy to hide in, wouldn't they? Look for any animals that may be making their home over there."

"Didn't Moses hide in the reeds when his mother put him in the river?"

"That's right! Great memory, Emma."

"I think I'd be really scared if I was a baby all alone in a basket on a river."

"Yes, but God had a pretty great plan for Moses, didn't He?"

LET'S LEARN FROM GOD'S WORD

After many years, so many of Jacob's descendants lived in Egypt that the ruler, Pharaoh, thought they would try to take his kingdom from him. He was starting to get worried—so worried that he told his people they should kill every Hebrew baby boy.

One Hebrew woman hid her baby boy in her house for three months. But soon he got so big that she was afraid people would notice him. So she did something daring to save him.

She made a basket out of reeds and covered it in tar so that it would float. She probably spent hours making sure this basket would keep her baby boy safe. Then she wrapped her baby up and gave him one last kiss good-bye. She pushed the basket into the current and watched it carry him down the river.

His big sister, Miriam, followed him. And do you know who saw the basket out of the water? The daughter of Pharaoh—the princess of Egypt! The princess saw the baby inside and decided she would be his new mother. But there was one problem: he needed to eat.

Miriam spoke up. "I know a woman who can feed him," she said.

So the princess sent Moses back to his very own mother, with money to pay her for feeding him and caring for him. When Moses was older, his mother took him to the princess to raise as her own. But it wouldn't be the last time Moses would see his family. One day he would rescue them and all of God's people from slavery and take them to the land God had set aside just for them.

"Do you think she was scared, Mom?"

"Who, sweetie?"

"Moses's sister. She had to come out of hiding to talk to the princess."

"Wow, you're right. I bet she was pretty scared."

"But she knew God was going to protect her, didn't she?"

"That's right, honey. God always has a plan."

HIDING GOD'S WORD IN YOUR HEART

What was something scary that you had to do for your family?

You, O LORD, will keep them;
   you will guard us from this generation forever. (Psalm 12:7)

Moses and the Burning, Talking Bush

Exodus 3

"I love campfires, don't you, Jackson?"

"Yes. But I'm tired from gathering wood. Doesn't it hurt your arm to cut all those logs? You must be really strong! Every time you whack a piece of wood, it goes, *Cra-a-ack*!"

"Ha-ha. Yes, check out these muscles. We'll need a lot of wood to keep the fire going all night long. It will go out if we don't add more logs to it. Jackson, have you ever heard the story of the burning bush and Moses?"

"No! Tell me, Grandma."

LET'S LEARN FROM GOD'S WORD

When Moses was a young man, he had trouble in Egypt, so he ran to the wilderness to hide from Pharaoh. One day while Moses was watching his father-in-law's sheep, he was near Mount Horeb. Everyone who lived nearby knew that Mount Horeb was God's mountain, and Moses was about to find out why. As he was walking by, Moses saw a bush on fire. But it wasn't burning up like logs on a bonfire. This bush was aflame with God's holiness.

Then God spoke to Moses: "Take off your shoes and stand back. This is holy ground. I am the God of your father, the God of Abraham, the God of Isaac, and the God of Jacob."

God told Moses that He saw the trouble His people were having in Egypt. God told Moses that he needed to go back to Egypt and tell Pharaoh that God wanted His people to be free.

Moses was terrified. How in the world would he do this?

But that's the thing: Moses wouldn't do it. God would do this *through* Moses. God led Moses faithfully, and Moses led God's people toward freedom. It was scary at times, and Moses didn't always do the right thing. In fact, sometimes he did the really wrong thing! But he loved God. He listened to God and His plans for His people. And boy, did God have plans for His people!

"Well, Jackson, it's time to go to bed."

"Thanks for telling me that story, Grandma."

"Anytime, my little man. God's holiness is such a lovely thing to rest in."

"Yes, and Moses sure had to trust in God. Did he get to see the new land for God's people?"

"Well, no, he died before that happened. But God did some amazing things during Moses's life. They were just plain miracles! But that's for a different night."

HIDING GOD'S WORD IN YOUR HEART

♥

What was something difficult that God asked you or your family to do?

You are my help and my deliverer. (Psalm 40:17)

Israel Escapes Slavery

Exodus 12–14

"Olivia, check out this huge river I just made. Isn't it cool?"

"Whoa! Look, I'm Moses and I'm going to lead the Israelites right through here."

"I'm coming behind you. Watch out, you Israelites! I'm Pharaoh and I'm going to get you!"

"No way, Jacob! God is on our side. There's no way you can catch us. Wait, here comes Dad!"

"Hey, kids, let's take a break and I'll fill you in on the whole story."

🌿 LET'S LEARN FROM GOD'S WORD

The night before they escaped Egypt, the people of God gathered in their homes, dressed and ready to leave the minute they got the word to go. They had a special meal of lamb, bread made without yeast, and bitter herbs. This was their first Passover meal.

They also painted blood from the lamb over their doors. An angel of death visited Egypt and killed every firstborn son but "passed over" the houses that had blood on their doorframes. The blood saved the oldest sons of those families.

That night so many Egyptians died that Pharaoh finally said to God's people, "Get out of my country." So they fled, quickly, in case Pharaoh changed his mind.

Soon the people stood on the shores of the Red Sea. But in the distance, the dust of Egyptian chariots rose into the air. Pharaoh was chasing them!

"What do we do now?" they asked Moses. "Did you bring us out here just to die?"

"No," Moses told them. "Don't you know God has a plan?"

God told Moses to raise his staff and stretch out his hands, and a strong wind rose over the water. It whipped and tossed the water back and forth until the water stood up on two sides and opened a pathway through the sea. The Israelites crossed over to safety on dry land.

But the chariots of Pharaoh were close behind. As soon as the last Israelite stepped onto the shore on the other side of the sea, Moses stretched out his hands once more. This time the water crashed back down on the Egyptian army. The Israelites watched the sea swallow up their enemy. God's people were safe. But they still had a long journey ahead of them.

"So, let's get back to the scene you guys were playing out."

"I'm God's people, crossing the Red Sea, and Jacob is the Egyptian army."

"Cool. Who's winning?"

"Me, of course."

"Actually, God was the winner, right? He's the One who had all the power to save His people."

"Yeah. I wish I could have seen that in real life. It must have been amazing."

"Me too. I bet that was one pretty cool day."

HIDING GOD'S WORD IN YOUR HEART

When did God make a way through a problem you were facing, when there didn't seem to be a way?

Save us and help us with your right hand,
that those you love may be delivered. (Psalm 60:5 NIV)

God Gives His People the Ten Commandments
Exodus 20

"Ooh, Kira. I love this new park!"

"It looks like so much fun, doesn't it, Bailey? Let's check out the rules before we start playing."

"Okay. It looks like they're mostly just here to keep us safe."

"I agree—no running up the slides, no pushing or shoving. Sounds good to me. Let's go!"

LET'S LEARN FROM GOD'S WORD

After God's people crossed the Red Sea, they were free. But they needed rules and laws for living, just like any other nation. Because God was their leader, those rules would come from Him.

God asked Moses to climb a mountain called Mount Sinai. Thunder and lightning lit up the sky on top of the mountain. The people down below saw it and were scared. But Moses walked right into the storm, where God was, and he spoke with God.

God gave Moses ten laws, written with His own finger onto stone tablets. Moses took these Ten Commandments back down to the people. This is what the laws said:

1. I am the LORD, and you should not worship any fake gods.
2. Do not make any idols, because I am the only true God.
3. Do not misuse God's name.
4. Rest on the Sabbath because God blessed it.
5. Honor your mom and dad, and your days in God's land will be long.
6. Do not murder.
7. Do not commit adultery.
8. Do not steal.
9. Do not lie.
10. Do not want what others have.

These are the rules that God's followers should know and do their best to live by. God promised His people that in every place where His people remember these laws, He would bless them.

Sometimes people think of the Ten Commandments as a burden because they remind us of things we do wrong. But the Ten Commandments are really a gift because they show us what life will be like in heaven, where there will be no more sin and where we will love one another and God perfectly.

"That's a lot to remember, Kira. I'm not sure I can follow all those rules."

"Bailey, you know what? When Jesus came, He said one law is greater than any other because it summarizes all the other laws. It's this: love the Lord your God with all your heart and with all your soul and with all your mind, and love your neighbor as yourself. That includes our 'neighbors' at the park while we play."

"Okay, Kira, I'll try my best!"

HIDING GOD'S WORD IN YOUR HEART

How can you love God and your family?

You shall love the Lord your God with all your heart and with all your soul and with all your mind. This is the great and first commandment. (Matthew 22:37–38)

God's People Worship the Golden Calf

Exodus 32

"Mom, I'm excited we got to visit Grandma and Grandpa again today."

"Me too, Jackson. It's such a lovely night to be out on the farm."

"Look at those cows in the field. They almost look like they're made of gold, the way the sun is shining on them."

"Wow, you're right, Jackson. That reminds me of the golden calf that God's people made. Do you know that story?"

🌿 LET'S LEARN FROM GOD'S WORD

While Moses was up on the mountain talking with God, the people started to worry that Moses had died up there. He was taking such a long time. Even though God had done amazing things they thought they would never, ever forget—like making a dry path through the middle of the Red Sea—the people actually forgot that God would take care of them. They went back to the old ways of Egypt and decided to make an idol to be their god instead of the one true God.

The people gathered the gold they'd brought with them from Egypt. They melted it and made a statue of a calf. And then they worshipped it.

When Moses finally did come down from the mountain, his face was shining from being in the presence of God. Moses saw the golden calf and became angry. Very, very angry, because the people of God had forgotten their one true God.

Moses took the stone tablets with the Ten Commandments written in God's own handwriting, and he threw them so hard that they broke. Then Moses took the golden calf and ground it down to powder. In fact, he scattered the powder all over the water, and he made the people drink it!

Moses wanted people who were going to be committed to God, so he asked them, "Who is on the LORD's side?" Anyone who didn't join God's side died. The rest of the people confessed that they'd been afraid and had forgotten God. They asked God for forgiveness.

God forgave the Israelites their sins. Soon it was time for them to set out again through the wilderness toward the Promised Land.

"Wow, after seeing the Red Sea split apart, why did the people get scared and forget about God?"

"Jackson, if I'm honest, I forget God's faithfulness a lot too. It's important for me to remember Him, especially when I get scared or impatient."

"Well, it doesn't look like it turns out too well when we take things into our own hands, Mom."

"Exactly."

HIDING GOD'S WORD IN YOUR HEART

Do you need to ask God for forgiveness today?

If we hope for what we do not see, we wait for it with patience.

(Romans 8:25)

God's People Enter the Promised Land

Joshua 6

"Olivia! What's the most epic battle ever? Go!"

"Okay, Jacob … that part in the book Dad read last night, where the good guys marched around a huge city. All they did was blow their horns and—"

"Yep, that's a good one, sis! It was all about trusting in God."

LET'S LEARN FROM GOD'S WORD

As God's people entered the Promised Land, they got quite a reputation. People heard about them and were scared because they knew these people didn't fight their battles alone. God fought for them.

For example, when God's people were camping outside the walls of Jericho, the people who lived in this city were terrified … except for a woman named Rahab. Earlier, she had helped some of God's people when they were spying on the city, and they had promised to keep her and her family safe when God attacked the city. In order to let them know which house was hers when they came back to attack, Rahab hung a red cord from her window.

Soon Joshua called all the fighting men of God forward and told God's unusual plan. For six days they would march around the city, blowing their horns all the way around the city walls. So that's what the Israelites did.

Finally, on the seventh day, they marched around the city again. And again. And again… Seven times. Then Joshua gave the signal. They yelled like they'd never yelled before. Loud and wild and crazy. Can you imagine the noise?

Inside Jericho the people panicked. And before they could even think, the city walls began to crumble and fall! The army of God's people took over the city. And the spies remembered Rahab; they led her and her family to safety in the camp of God's people.

Rahab's story didn't end there. This brave woman who feared God, even though she was from Jericho, became an ancestor of King David. You see, God's plan was at work.

"You guys must be the mighty army of Israel, about to destroy Jericho."

"Dad, you're right! I'm one of the spies, so I have to go in and save Rahab."

"That's an amazing story, isn't it? We can't always see God's plan, but He always has one."

"Yes, Dad! That's why we have to trust Him, Olivia, even when we aren't sure what He's doing."

HIDING GOD'S WORD IN YOUR HEART

Why do you think we can't always see God's plan?

Trust in the LORD with all your heart;
    do not depend on your own understanding. (Proverbs 3:5 NLT)

Deborah: A Mighty Warrior Woman

Judges 4–5

"Whoo! Look, Kira! I'm going so high!"

"Wow, Bailey. Be careful up there. You're getting too high."

"I'm not scared. Whoo!"

"Well, good … I guess. You know, you're reminding me of a fearless woman in the Old Testament: Deborah."

✎ LET'S LEARN FROM GOD'S WORD

So far we've heard mostly about mighty men of God. And we just heard about Rahab. Now we are going to hear about another strong and valiant woman. Her name was Deborah.

Remember back in Noah's day when people forgot that God had created them to enjoy Him and to glorify Him with their lives? Well, that happened again. In fact, it happened a lot. But when Deborah was alive, they forgot God's laws so much that they were captured by an evil king named Jabin.

Deborah was a prophetess. That means she heard the voice of God and told the people of God what He said. She was also a judge over Israel. Both men and women came to her to hear what God wanted them to do.

God spoke to Deborah and told her that His people should prepare to go to war against King Jabin and his general, Sisera. When Deborah told the people, they said they would go, but only if she came too. She must have been one powerful woman.

So Deborah led God's people to the battlefield, and she and her men were so fierce that Sisera and his army ran away.

The funny thing is, Sisera sneaked away to the tent of a woman he thought was his friend, but while he rested from the battle, she killed him and turned his body over to Deborah's army.

In a time when men usually were the rulers, God used two women to accomplish his plan. Pretty amazing, don't you think?

"Bailey, it's time to go."

"Okay. Bye, you guys! Kira, I sure love this park. It's so close to school, and I can't wait to play like a fearless warrior again!"

HIDING GOD'S WORD IN YOUR HEART

You are part of God's plan too. How will you know when God is calling you to help Him with His plans?

Be strong and courageous. (Joshua 1:9)

Samson: God's Strong Man

Judges 16

"Whoa, boy. Hi there, Jackson! Did you come to watch the horses work?"

"Yes, Grandpa. Wow, they're strong."

"Hop up here next to me on the wagon. You can see them better up here."

"Thanks! I've never seen anything that can pull such a heavy load. They're like Samson in the Bible. He was one of the strongest men ever, right?"

"That's right! Do you know his story?"

LET'S LEARN FROM GOD'S WORD

Samson was another mighty man whom God used as part of His plans. In fact, Samson was one of the strongest men who ever lived. Before he was born, an angel appeared to Samson's mom and told her things that she and her husband must do to show that Samson was God's special man, set apart for His purpose. Samson's parents listened to God and did as He said, and Samson became a judge over God's people.

The Philistines were enemies of God's people. They did not believe in the one true God and were constantly fighting with God's people, including Samson. They wanted to know what made him so strong. So they sent a woman—a beautiful woman named Delilah—to find out. (Just so you know, the secret was his long hair, which he should never, ever cut.)

Delilah pretended to be Samson's friend. Samson went to visit her at her house. She asked him three times to tell her what his secret was. He made up fake answers to trick her, but she kept trying. One time she tied ropes around him

while he was sleeping, but when he woke up, he broke the ropes like they were spaghetti noodles.

Delilah pretended to cry and mope around, trying to make Samson feel guilty. You'd think by now that Samson would know not to trust her, right? Wrong. The fourth time Delilah asked what his secret was, he told her the truth.

So Delilah lulled Samson to sleep and had a man cut off his hair. Then she started screaming that the Philistines were coming. When Samson woke up, he realized his strength was gone. The Philistines captured him and he lived as a prisoner for the rest of his life.

But as his hair began to grow back, his strength did too. One day the Philistines brought Samson to a temple where they were having a celebration and worshipping fake gods. Samson prayed to the Lord to give him strength one last time. God answered his prayer. Samson pushed with all his might against two pillars that were holding up the temple. He pushed and pushed, and finally the temple came crashing down on all the people.

"God's design is for these horses to be strong workers. But if they were to start prancing around to show off how strong they are, they wouldn't be useful anymore."

"So Samson could use his strength as long as he was following God's laws? But once he decided he could do it without God, he lost his strength?"

"That's right! Now let's get these horses in the barn and go eat."

HIDING GOD'S WORD IN YOUR HEART

When has God helped you do something you didn't think you could do?

I can do all things through him who strengthens me.

(Philippians 4:13)

Ruth: The Faithful Daughter-in-Law

Ruth 1–4

"Aw, Emma, look. Isn't he adorable?"

"He's so tiny! Can I hold him?"

"Sure! Sit here and we'll help you. Oh, Emma, you look like such a big girl with your cousin in your arms. Now our family name will go on to the next generation."

"What does that mean?"

"Well, my precious granddaughter, it means that if your little cousin here has children of his own someday, our last name will keep on going. You know, that reminds me of the story of Ruth, a young woman in the Bible."

🪶 LET'S LEARN FROM GOD'S WORD

Ruth grew up in an area called Moab. This wasn't part of God's Promised Land. Ruth was an outsider. But God had a plan to change that.

When she grew up, Ruth married the son of an Israelite woman named Naomi. She became part of his family. Another woman married Naomi's other son. But when Naomi's husband and their two sons died, the three wives were left alone. Naomi told her daughters-in-law to return to their own families, and she would go back to her home in Israel by herself.

Ruth knew it would be easier to go back to her own home, but she decided to go with Naomi instead. In this very brave moment, she knew it was more important for her to follow the God Naomi worshipped, the only true God, than to stay in Moab and worship false gods.

When Naomi and Ruth got to Israel, they looked for food and a place to stay. God provided a relative of Naomi's, named Boaz, to take care of the two women. Boaz had heard that Ruth was a good woman who was taking care of her mother-in-law. After seeing her hard work collecting food and her never-give-up attitude, Boaz decided to marry Ruth.

Even when it seems like God has forgotten about us, it turns out He has a plan. Do you know who Ruth's great-grandson was? King David. And many, many years after that, Jesus was born into this same family. Because of Ruth's faithfulness and God's great plan, wonderful things came out of this hard time for Ruth and Naomi.

"It was fun to see the baby, wasn't it, Emma?"

"Yeah, I'm so glad I got to hold him. Mom, do you ever get sad you didn't have a son who would keep our last name going?"

"Not at all, sweetie! Jesus gave me you, and He has a beautiful plan for you and me. And I get to enjoy the sweetness of your cousin too. What a gift!"

HIDING GOD'S WORD IN YOUR HEART

How have you seen God's plan in your own life? What amazing things has He done for your family so far?

I am the root and the descendant of David, the bright morning star.

(Revelation 22:16)

Samuel: The Boy Who Heard God's Voice
1 Samuel 3

"Dad, have you ever heard God's voice? Really heard His voice, like He was talking to you out loud?"

"No, Jacob, I haven't. Not out loud. But people in the Bible did hear His voice at times."

"Who, Dad?"

"Well, Olivia, Samuel heard God speak to him."

"What did He say?"

 LET'S LEARN FROM GOD'S WORD

Samuel was a young boy who grew up in a temple with a priest named Eli. One night, while Samuel was sleeping, he heard a voice calling him: "Samuel!"

Samuel thought Eli had called him. So he jumped up and ran to Eli's room, woke him up, and asked what he wanted.

Eli was confused. He hadn't called Samuel. So Eli sent Samuel back to bed.

This happened two more times. At that point, Eli realized that God was calling Samuel. He said, "Go back to bed, and if God calls again, say, 'Here I am, Lord. What do You want to say to me?'"

Sure enough, when Samuel went back to bed, God called him. When God chooses a person to be a part of His plan, He doesn't give up! He keeps on calling us until we figure it out.

72

When God spoke to Samuel, He had a warning for Israel. Hard things were coming for them, but it was all part of His big plan. They would have to trust Him awhile longer before they'd be able to see what He had in store for them. And Samuel would also be part of God's plan to lead the people and point them to God.

"Samuel was finally able to hear God's voice because he was ready to listen for it, right, Jacob and Olivia?"

"Yes, Dad! Once he knew it was God speaking to him, everything made sense."

"That's right. So be listening for God to speak to you too. You never know what He might have planned for you. Now go pick out the cereal you want and listen for my voice too. Meet me at the checkout when I call you!"

Jacob!
Olivia!

HIDING GOD'S WORD IN YOUR HEART

How would you respond if you heard God's voice today?

My sheep hear my voice, and I know them, and they follow me.

(John 10:27)

David: The Boy Who Fought a Giant

1 Samuel 17

"Bye, Emma! Have an awesome day!"

"Byyyeee, baby Emma. Have an awesome-wawsome day, baby Emma. Why does your mom come to the bus stop every day, Emma? Are you scared to go to school?"

"No, I'm not scared. She just wants to say bye."

"Well, tell her to quit or everyone's going to think you're a baby."

Ugh, I wish Mom would drive me to school. And I wish that big bully would just leave me alone. Why is she picking on me? This is so unfair.

LET'S LEARN FROM GOD'S WORD

God's people were again facing their worst enemy, the Philistines. The Philistines had sent their best fighter out to beat God's people. He was a giant of a man named Goliath. He was taunting the army of God and the king of Israel.

"Come out and fight like men!" yelled Goliath. "If you win, we will be your slaves. But if I win, you will be our slaves!" How could he not win, as big as he was?

The Israelites were scared. They wondered if God had forgotten about His promise to keep them safe. But the shepherd boy David knew God hadn't forgotten. He remembered that God had a plan. David said he would fight Goliath, even though he was a boy. After all, he had fought lions and bears before when he was watching and protecting his sheep. And he knew that God was with him.

David took five smooth pebbles from a river bed, put his slingshot in his hand, and headed toward Goliath. Of course, the giant mocked him. But David said, "You come with a sword, but I come in the name of the LORD, the God of the armies of Israel. The LORD will deliver you into my hand." David swung his slingshot around and landed a stone smack in the middle of Goliath's forehead. The giant fell down dead. Israel won!

Although Goliath was big, God was even bigger. God is always bigger than anything His people face.

"Mom, sometimes I just wish there were no bullies."

"Emma, what bullies?"

"Oh, this girl makes fun of me at the bus stop. She says you shouldn't go with me every day like you do."

"Hmm, well, we can't let her stop us from doing what we like to do. God loves us, and He's bigger than any problem we have."

"How about we both wave to her tomorrow and tell her to have a great day at school?"

"Perfect idea, Emma! And just know that as long as you want me to be there with you at the bus stop, I will be there."

HIDING GOD'S WORD IN YOUR HEART

Why do you think it is tempting to bully other people?

If God is for us, who can be against us? (Romans 8:31)

Solomon: The King Who Built God's Temple

1 Kings 6; 2 Chronicles 3

"Kira, you wouldn't believe our field trip today. It was *amazing!*"

"Well, tell me all about it. I can't wait to hear!"

"We went to this awesome museum and there were real royal jewels from old kings and queens there. It was the coolest thing ever. I've never been that close to a real crown before."

"Wow, that does sound cool. It makes me think of King Solomon in the Bible and all his riches."

LET'S LEARN FROM GOD'S WORD

Do you remember David, the shepherd boy who killed giant Goliath? Well, David grew up to be king over Israel. When King David died, his son Solomon became the king. Solomon was the wisest person in the land. (That means he had really good ideas for solving problems and understanding things.)

One thing King David had really, really wanted to do was build God a special building called a temple. But God told David that wasn't his job. It would be Solomon's job.

Once Solomon's kingdom was running smoothly, he started to make plans for building God's temple in the city of Jerusalem. Special wood was shipped in from a nearby country called Lebanon. The best and most skilled artists came to Jerusalem to begin making the art that would fill the temple. They made sculptures of flowers, palm trees, and angels.

When it was finished, every part of the temple—every floor, every sculpture, every table, every wall, *everything*—was covered with gold. Can you imagine what that building must have looked like? As the sun set in the evening, the light reflected off all that gold. The temple gleamed and sparkled, reminding Israel of God's great glory!

Important people—other kings and queens—came from all over the world to meet Solomon and see the temple he had built. But all the fame and attention kind of went to his head. By the end of his life he was unhappy. He had made the choice to enjoy riches and fame instead of enjoying God and glorifying Him. So even though Solomon had great wisdom, he'd forgotten that the only way to be truly happy was to put the one true God first.

"Kira, even though Solomon was wise, he still forgot to enjoy God and glorify Him?"

"Yep. When life is going really well, sometimes it's hard to remember you need God."

"Will you please always remind me that I need God?"

"Of course. And you do the same for me. We can help each other."

HIDING GOD'S WORD IN YOUR HEART

Why do you always need God?

Seek first the kingdom of God and his righteousness, and all these things will be added to you. (Matthew 6:33)

Elijah: The Man Who Tested the Gods

1 Kings 18

"Hey, Bailey, slow down! What's going on? Why are you crying?"

"Kira, those kids were being so mean. They're bothering me because I'm a Christian. I wanted to fight back, but I decided to just leave. I didn't want a fight. Still, I wish they wouldn't bully me like that. It hurts."

"Do you remember the story I told you about Elijah in the Bible and how the people teased him for following God too?"

LET'S LEARN FROM GOD'S WORD

Elijah was a prophet during a time when almost no one followed God. Israel had almost completely forgotten about Him because so many people thought their fake, made-up gods were better than the only true God. Elijah's job was to tell people the truth, but it was really hard to get people to believe him. They just wouldn't listen.

So Elijah had an idea: he would have a contest to see whose God was the best. Who do you think won? Well, let's not spoil the ending. It's a pretty exciting story.

Elijah told the people who worshipped the fake god called Baal to cut up a dead bull and put it on an altar, just like they normally did for sacrifices. But instead of starting a fire like usual, they would ask *Baal* to start the fire. Elijah would also prepare a sacrifice, and he would ask *God* to start the fire.

The prophets of Baal—all 450 of them—went first. They cried and danced and did all sorts of nonsense to get Baal to respond. But, of course, since Baal was not real, nothing happened.

Then it was Elijah's turn. Before he asked God to light the sacrifice with holy fire, he poured three big buckets of water on the altar. He wanted to make it clear that when fire came it wouldn't be a trick. It would come from God alone.

And it did! When that fire came down, it didn't just burn up the meat and the wood. It burned the stones and dust and even licked up the water that filled the trench around it. God's holy fire was all consuming, and the people stood in awe. They knew without a doubt that God is real and that He is the one true God.

"Wow, that's really amazing. How could you not believe in God after you saw that?"

"Bailey, you know what else is amazing? It says later in the Bible that Elijah never died. God just took him up to heaven in a whirlwind. Pretty cool."

"If God can do those awesome, powerful things and if He loves me and protects me, I can ask Him to help me with those bullies."

"You sure can! And don't forget about me. I can help too!"

HIDING GOD'S WORD IN YOUR HEART

♥

Describe a time when you've been bullied. How can God help? How can others help?

Once God has spoken;
    twice have I heard this:
that power belongs to God. (Psalm 62:11)

Esther: The Woman Who Saved God's People

Esther 1–10

"Aunt Maria, I love this dress! I feel so beautiful."

"You look beautiful, Emma! You know, I was just reading the story of Esther in my Bible this morning, and now you're reminding me of her."

"How can a sparkly dress remind you of a Bible story? Didn't people wear old, boring clothes back then?"

"Oh no. Esther was one of the most beautiful women in the country of Persia. She had all the makeup, jewelry, and fancy dresses she wanted. But what made her beautiful had nothing to do with her clothes."

🖋 LET'S LEARN FROM GOD'S WORD

King Xerxes ruled over the land from Egypt all the way to India in Asia. He lived in a beautiful palace with marble pillars, curtains made from the finest linen, and floors that were a beautiful pattern of precious stones. Because of his great wealth and power, he expected everyone to do whatever he asked. Many people were afraid of him.

This king wanted a wife, so he did what any rich king would do. He sent for the most beautiful women in the kingdom to come to his palace. They were given spa treatments to make them even prettier and lessons on how to act like a princess. Eventually the king picked his favorite—a woman named Esther—and made her the queen. (By the way, he didn't know she was Jewish.)

One day, when Esther's cousin Mordecai was sitting by the city gates, he overheard two men plotting to kill the king. Mordecai told Esther, and Esther warned the king and saved his life.

Sometime later, the king's adviser, Haman, was plotting to kill Esther's people, the Jews. Mordecai begged Esther to go before the king and ask him to spare her people. The only problem was that *no one* was allowed to go before the king without his permission.

Esther was scared—really scared. She had seen what happened to people who didn't follow the king's rules. But God was preparing her to be the one who would save the Jews. Esther prayed, asking for God's blessing on this dangerous mission.

God blessed Esther's obedience. When King Xerxes heard of Haman's awful plan, he had *Haman* killed instead of the Jews. Because Esther trusted God's plan, even when she didn't know for sure where He was leading, her people were saved.

"I'm not sure I could be that brave, Aunt Maria."

"I know you trust God to take care of you, Emma, no matter what happens. Let's pray that God will deliver you through anything that's sad or scary or frustrating: *Dear God, You promise to deliver us from all evil. Please be with us when scary things happen, and help us to remember that You are always, always in charge. We love You. Thank You for being our Daddy.*"

HIDING GOD'S WORD IN YOUR HEART

Call upon me in the day of trouble;
   I will deliver you, and you shall glorify me. (Psalm 50:15)

Songs to Praise God

Job 37

"Look at the stars, Grandpa. There are so many out tonight!"

"I bet you can't see all these stars, Jackson, from the big city where you live."

"Nope. I've never seen so many stars in my life."

"You know, God made each one of those stars. He knew exactly where He wanted each one to go in the sky."

"I think He's made a beautiful sparkling picture up there."

"He sure has, Jackson. It reminds me of how a man named Job looked up to God even when he faced hard times. No matter what, Job trusted that God knew exactly what He was doing."

LET'S LEARN FROM GOD'S WORD

There was a man in the Old Testament named Job (it rhymes with *globe*). He loved God, but God allowed him to lose everything that had ever been important to him—his children, his money, his health. Everything.

But he still had God. And he still wanted to enjoy God and glorify Him.

Job was very, very sad for a long time. Then God spoke to him. He reminded Job that He's in control of everything—like those stars we see up in the sky and the bears that hibernate for the winter. He made the volcanoes and decides when

the lava will flow out of them. God chose the colors we see in spring flowers, and He put the slimiest snakes in their river beds. It's His choice when the clouds become thick with rain and lightning flashes across the sky.

Can you make a cloud in the sky?

Can you make a caterpillar turn into a butterfly?

No, only God can do these things. He is amazing, powerful, and good.

"I'd really never thought about that before, Grandpa. I mean, I knew that the clouds and the mountains and butterflies had to get here somehow. I just never thought about how God is the only One who could make them!"

"Yep, Jackson—and what's really cool is that the God who is so powerful and made these majestic things knows your name. He loves you very much!"

"Wow."

HIDING GOD'S WORD IN YOUR HEART

♥

What are some of your favorite things that God has made?

Stop and consider the wondrous works of God. (Job 37:14)

The Shepherd's Prayer
Psalm 23

"Jackson, can you see Grandpa whistling to our dog, Beau? He does that to tell him where to go so he'll get the sheep in the barn as fast as he can."

"I think the storm is scary, but it doesn't seem to bother Grandpa at all."

"You know, Jackson, I think Grandpa's brave because he knows the Good Shepherd is watching out for him, the same way Grandpa's watching out for those sheep. Have you heard about Psalm 23 in the Bible? It's called the shepherd's psalm."

LET'S LEARN FROM GOD'S WORD

The LORD is my shepherd; I shall not want.
    He makes me lie down in green pastures.
He leads me beside still waters.
    He restores my soul.
He leads me in paths of righteousness
    for his name's sake.

Even though I walk through the valley of the shadow of death,
    I will fear no evil,
for you are with me;
    your rod and your staff,
    they comfort me.

You prepare a table before me
    in the presence of my enemies;
you anoint my head with oil;
    my cup overflows.
Surely goodness and mercy shall follow me
    all the days of my life,
and I shall dwell in the house of the LORD
    forever. (Psalm 23)

"Grandma, do you think the sheep are afraid of the storm?"

"Oh, not at all. They don't need to be afraid. They know their shepherd is watching over them."

HIDING GOD'S WORD IN YOUR HEART

What is one way you could remember God is with you when you are scared?

The LORD is my shepherd; I shall not want. (Psalm 23:1)

Holy Is the Lord God Almighty

Isaiah 6

"Dad, can we talk?"

"Sure, Jacob. What's up?"

"Well, I think I did something bad at school today. I was trying to make the other kids like me, so I made fun of my friend Corey when he fell down in PE. He's not very good at running. But instead of helping him, I laughed at him. I feel really bad."

"Hmmm, that's hard. Let me tell you a story that might help."

LET'S LEARN FROM GOD'S WORD

Isaiah had a really interesting life. The king of Israel died after ruling the country for over fifty years. What was going to happen to the country now? God spoke to Isaiah and showed him glimpses of heaven. Isaiah told God's people about what he saw of heaven to remind them to be faithful to God, their ultimate ruler.

One day Isaiah was praying when suddenly he saw the Lord sitting on a throne. God was way high up in the air, and He was wearing a long robe that filled the whole temple. It was amazing!

Above God two angels were flying. They each had six wings. Two wings covered their faces and two wings covered their feet. They used the other two wings to fly. The angels were calling back and forth to each other, "Holy, holy, holy is the LORD of hosts; the whole earth is full of His glory!"

Isaiah was stunned. He'd never seen anything so wonderful in his life. But the only thing he could think about was how sinful he was. He cried to God, "I'm a sinner. I am not worthy to see this." (In other words, Isaiah didn't feel like he should have the privilege of actually seeing God this way.)

But God reached out, touched Isaiah, and told him that he'd been forgiven.

"You know how dirty with grease I get when I fix stuff here in the garage? And how I need to clean up before dinner? Well, our sins cover us up with dirty muck, just like that grease on my hands."

"So how do you get rid of sins, Dad?"

"Well, by asking for God's forgiveness. He reaches out and touches us, and our hearts are totally clean again."

"Dad, I'm so sorry. I really messed up. Will you forgive me?"

"Of course. But you know what? You need to ask God for forgiveness too. Want me to help?"

"Yes, will you pray with me?"

HIDING GOD'S WORD IN YOUR HEART

♥

Will you ask God for forgiveness today?

Behold … your guilt is taken away, and your sin atoned for. (Isaiah 6:7)

God's People Are Homeless

Jeremiah 29:4–14

"Kira, why don't those people go home? It's so cold out here."

"Well, Bailey, I don't think they have a home. They're just trying to get through the day and have a meal to eat."

"They don't have a home? That's really sad."

"Yeah, it is. Did you know even God's people were homeless for a while? Their land was invaded by an enemy army. They had to go live in a foreign country as slaves."

103

LET'S LEARN FROM GOD'S WORD

God's people of Israel had been living in the Promised Land for a long time. They had built cities and had children and grandchildren there. It was home. But they had forgotten to enjoy and glorify God there. They had forgotten to worship Him and praise Him for all He had done in their lives. God gave them many chances to turn back to Him, and He warned them through prophets, but they just didn't listen.

So God allowed them to go through a very hard time. Nebuchadnezzar, king of Babylon, attacked Jerusalem. He took many of the people to Babylon, even though they didn't want to go there.

Babylon was far, far away from Jerusalem and the home they loved. It was a different country with a different language, different food, and different ways of doing things. The Israelites were slaves in a foreign land. They were uncomfortable and unhappy. And worse, they couldn't leave.

Then God gave them strange instructions: "Build houses. Plant gardens. Do good things in Babylon. Pray for the city and make it a great place to live."

God would eventually take His people back to Jerusalem. Until then, He wanted the people to love the city. "Because I have a plan for you," God said, "a plan to help you, not to hurt you. Trust Me. Good things will come of this."

"Kira, I'd like to do something to make our city better. Maybe we could fix dinner and take it down to that family."

"That's a great idea. Let's make some sandwiches and grab some bags of chips."

"And maybe we could stop and get some orange juice too."

"Yes! God is so good to provide for us. Let's share that with others."

HIDING GOD'S WORD IN YOUR HEART

♥

What you can do to help your community, or how can you volunteer to help others?

"I know the plans I have for you," says the LORD. "They are plans for good and not for disaster, to give you a future and a hope."

(Jeremiah 29:11 NLT)

Daniel: The Man the Lions Wouldn't Attack

Daniel 6

Arroooo. Arrooo.

"What's that noise, Grandpa? It sounds close!"

"Don't worry. It's just a few coyotes on that hill. They're saying good night."

"Will the chickens be okay?"

"Yes. We're going to lock them up tight in the barn."

"Okay. I still don't really like that noise."

"You know, Jackson, there was a man in the Bible named Daniel. God protected him from some wild animals."

LET'S LEARN FROM GOD'S WORD

Another group of people, the Persians, had taken over Babylon, and Daniel was taken away to serve their king named Darius. Many Persians were jealous of him. Daniel had followed God's commands to love that city, and he was serving as an adviser to the king, who was named Darius. Daniel's position was really powerful. Many Babylonians were jealous of him. Some even tried to get him in trouble.

Some of these men went to King Darius and said, "Great and honorable king, we suggest that you make a rule that everyone shall pray only to you. All you have to do is sign this paper and it will become law."

King Darius didn't know God. Even though he was Daniel's friend, these men tricked him. By signing this law, the king made it illegal to pray to God in Persia.

Do you think Daniel quit praying? No, he didn't.

And so even though Daniel had worked hard to make Persia a good place to live, the king had to punish him for breaking the law. The punishment was to be thrown into a pit of lions!

The jealous men were happy. Their plan had worked! They hoped the lions would eat Daniel up. But God had a different plan.

After pacing all night, the worried king came back to the pit in the morning to check on Daniel. To his great surprise, the king discovered that Daniel was still alive! God had shut the lions' mouths so they didn't hurt Daniel. King Darius saw how God helped his friend. And he made a new law for his kingdom: "From now on, people will worship the God of Daniel, the living and one true God. His kingdom will never be destroyed. God will always be our King!"

"Grandpa, if we had a law where we weren't allowed to pray, would you pray anyway? Even if it meant those coyotes would come and hurt you?"

"Jackson, I know this: God is with those who love Him, and He helps us face any challenge. He gives us the strength to believe in Him. It doesn't come from ourselves. So we should pray every day to be brave and do the right thing."

"Grandpa, will you pray for me to be brave like you are?"

"I already do, Jackson. Every day. And you *are* brave, by the way."

HIDING GOD'S WORD IN YOUR HEART

♥

What would you do if someone said you weren't allowed to pray?

Be joyful in hope, patient in affliction, faithful in prayer. (Romans 12:12 NIV)

Jonah: The Runaway Prophet

Jonah 1–4

"Ack! Jacob, I think a fish just nibbled my toe! That's so gross."

"We're in a lake, Olivia. Of course they're going to nibble you. But they won't hurt you. They're tiny."

"Remember that story Dad told us about Jonah, the prophet who got eaten by a whale? Can you even imagine? Yuck."

"I wonder what it was like inside his tummy. He was there for three days!"

"No way—that's not even possible! Oh, hi, Dad!"

"With God, all things are possible, kids. Let me tell you the story again."

LET'S LEARN FROM GOD'S WORD

If God's people of Israel had one enemy they really, really couldn't stand, it was Assyria. The people in Assyria were mean, scary, and didn't love God. Israel wanted God to make them disappear.

But then God told an Israelite named Jonah to go to Nineveh, the capital city of Assyria. He told Jonah to tell the people that if they asked for forgiveness, God would forgive their sins.

Jonah was angry. "Why, God? They are evil people who don't love or serve You."

Instead of heading across the desert toward Assyria, Jonah hopped on a boat going the opposite direction. He wasn't going to do what God asked him to do. He was going to run away instead.

But the thing is, you can't run away from God.

A big storm came up. Waves crashed against the boat. The other men on board were scared. "Who is God angry at?" they asked.

Jonah finally did the right thing. "God's angry with me," he told them. "Throw me overboard."

But God still had a plan. That plan was for Jonah to tell the people in Nineveh about God's forgiveness. God sent a giant fish to swallow Jonah so he wouldn't drown. Three days later the fish threw up Jonah onto the beach. Can you imagine the nasty gunk that must have been on his clothes and hair? But he was ready to preach God's good news to Nineveh.

The people of Nineveh asked for God's forgiveness. God saved them from destruction because Jonah did what God asked.

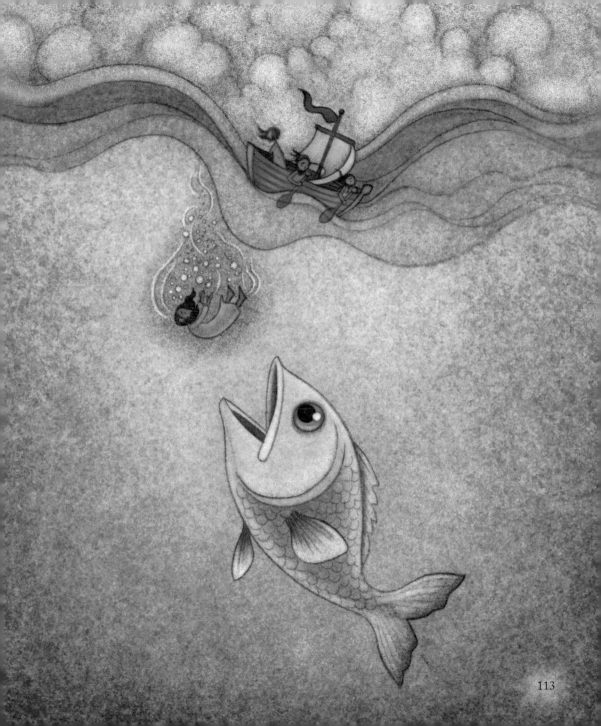

"Dad, does God forgive us all the time? Even when we don't do what He asks us to do?"

"Absolutely. We have all sinned. But Jesus lived a completely perfect life. He told His Father that He would die instead of us so that we can be forgiven and live with God forever. It's pretty amazing, isn't it?"

HIDING GOD'S WORD IN YOUR HEART

Why do you think God gave Jonah a second chance?

The LORD is merciful and gracious,
    slow to anger and abounding in steadfast love. (Psalm 103:8)

Jesus Is Coming!

Micah 5:2

"It's snowing! And it's going to be Christmas soon. I'm so excited. I can't wait! It always seems like Christmas takes so long to get here, but I guess that's part of what makes it so fun."

"The Israelites had to wait a long time for Christmas too. They were slaves for almost four hundred years before Jesus was born. That's a really long time to wait."

LET'S LEARN FROM GOD'S WORD

For many years the people of Israel lived as slaves in Babylon. They missed their home. They missed their freedom. Would they ever be able to go back home? Was God listening? Did He see them, like long ago when they were slaves in Egypt? Would God rescue them again? They longed for the Messiah to come. Their prophets had been talking about the Messiah for a long time!

In fact, way back in the garden of Eden, God had a plan for the Savior to come. And throughout time, God's people had been waiting for Him. Abraham and Isaac and Jacob had waited for Him. King David and King Solomon had waited for Him. Isaiah had waited for Him. But He hadn't come yet.

"When will He come, God?" the people of Israel asked. "You've promised One who will be a powerful king. One who will love us and save us from this hard, hard life. We're ready for Him—now!"

It was almost time. That first Christmas wasn't too far away. They just had to wait a little longer … only four hundred more years or so. But in the meantime, they *did* get to go back home. It wasn't the same. The amazing, dazzling temple that Solomon had built had been destroyed. And his gorgeous palace too. Even the walls around the city were gone, with just crumbles of stone here and there. And so, while God's people waited for their Savior to come, they rebuilt their city of Jerusalem. It was never as wonderful as it once was, but it was their home, and it felt so good to be home again. And so God's people waited. And watched. And waited.

"What are you hoping to get this Christmas, Bailey?"

"I want my very own Bible for Christmas. A big-kid Bible I can study by myself."

"That's a wonderful idea, Bailey!"

"Brrr, it's cold. Maybe we should make some hot chocolate at home?"

"You know what, that's another wonderful idea. Let's go!"

HIDING GOD'S WORD IN YOUR HEART

♥

Why is waiting so hard? What about when we're waiting for God's promises?

For to us a child is born,
   to us a son is given,
   and the government will be on his shoulders.
And he will be called
   Wonderful Counselor, Mighty God,
   Everlasting Father, Prince of Peace.
   (Isaiah 9:6 NIV)

The Savior Is Born

Matthew 1:18–25; Luke 2

"Mom, do you like my costume?"

"That's right! Tonight's the night of our church Christmas program. And, you look wonderful, Emma! Who's that you're holding?"

"This is going to be baby Jesus. It's really my doll Claire, but we're hiding her hair in the swaddling clothes."

"Ah, good idea. Isn't it amazing that Jesus came down to earth as a baby just to save you and me?"

🖋 LET'S LEARN FROM GOD'S WORD

Mary lived in a town called Nazareth. Her parents had found a husband for her: Joseph, a carpenter. But God had even more special plans for Mary.

One day the most unexpected thing happened. An angel appeared to Mary. "Greetings, favored one! The Lord is with you!" he told her.

Mary was surprised. She was just a girl from a small town. But the angel was bringing her a message from God Himself: she was going to have a child, a baby boy. That boy would be the Son of God! His name would be Jesus.

Mary didn't know what to think. She didn't understand. *I'm just a young girl and I'm not even married yet*, she thought. But just as the angel said, the Spirit of God visited Mary, and she became pregnant with Jesus.

When Joseph found out, he was horrified. The person he was going to marry was pregnant? It was shameful. So he decided not to marry her after all. That's when

120

an angel visited him and told him of God's bigger, better plan. Joseph believed the angel. He married Mary and together they waited for Jesus to be born.

Then the emperor, Caesar Augustus, said everyone had to go to the town their ancestors were from to be counted. Joseph was from the town of Bethlehem, so he and Mary had to take a road trip. By that time, Mary was very, very pregnant.

It was a long journey. When they arrived in Bethlehem, the town was very crowded. Mary and Joseph had nowhere to stay, except for a dirty stable with animals in it. There, Mary gave birth to Jesus. She wrapped Him in cloths and put Him in a manger to sleep. She was probably tired and scared. This wasn't how she would have written her story. But God's story was bigger, better, and more beautiful than any Mary could have imagined.

"And she gave birth to her firstborn son and wrapped him in swaddling cloths and laid him in a manger, because there was no place for them in the inn" (Luke 2:7).

"Welcome, baby Jesus. We're so very glad You're here."

HIDING GOD'S WORD IN YOUR HEART

What do you like best about Christmas?

Unto you is born this day in the city of David a Savior, who is Christ the Lord. And this will be a sign for you: you will find a baby wrapped in swaddling cloths and lying in a manger. (Luke 2:11–12)

The Shepherds and the Angels

Luke 2

"Grandma, what are those strange lights out there? I've never seen those before."

"Those are the Northern Lights. Aren't they beautiful?"

"Do you think that's what the sky looked like when the angels came to sing to the shepherds when Jesus was born?"

"With all those angels in the sky, Jackson, I imagine that night the sky was even more beautiful than this."

LET'S LEARN FROM GOD'S WORD

It had started just like every other day. The shepherds led the sheep from the farm up into the hills to get good food where the fresh grass grew. They'd been there for a few hours and had just finished their dinner. The men sat around the fire and told stories of the ancient faith—the stories their grandfathers' grandfathers had

told about the God of Abraham, Isaac, and Jacob … and how He was going to send a Messiah.

That's when they sat up with a jolt. Were their eyes playing tricks on them? Some figure was floating up in the sky. Could it be … an angel? Yes, there, look—another one.

Soon the sky was filled with angels. And the music! It was unlike anything they'd ever heard before: "Glory to God in the highest, and peace on earth to all! Tonight a Savior has been born for you. His name is Christ the Lord. Rejoice!"

It didn't take long for the shepherds to go and see this new baby! All the way down the hill, as they walked through the city to find Jesus, they couldn't wait to see their Savior. The one they had heard about was finally here!"

When they arrived, they knelt down before baby Jesus. Mary and Joseph weren't sure what to do—this was all so new to them. But the shepherds told them about the angels, the song, and the promise that God was going to bring peace to everyone.

Mary held her baby tight. She thought and thought and thought about all she'd heard. It was all quite marvelous.

"Grandma, I wish I could have been there with the shepherds to hear the angels singing that night."

"Yes, me too. It must have been amazing."

"Maybe God gives us the Northern Lights so we'll always remember that night."

"Well, I think that's a fabulous way to remember it, Jackson."

HIDING GOD'S WORD IN YOUR HEART

What reminders does God give you about the night Jesus was born?

Glory to God in the highest,
    and on earth peace among those with whom he is pleased!

(Luke 2:14)

The Wise Men Come

Matthew 2:1–12

"What did you get, Bailey?"

"It's just what I wanted—my very own Bible. Thanks, Kira. I love it."

"Why don't you read us a story? How about the part where the wise men bring gifts to Jesus? That's a good story to read today!"

🖋 LET'S LEARN FROM GOD'S WORD

Far, far away from Jerusalem, some very wise men—people who were smart and studied a lot—decided to go and celebrate the new King of the Jews.

So they did. They followed the star to Jesus. It took them a long time because they had to ride on camels instead of in an airplane, but they eventually arrived in Jerusalem, at the palace of King Herod. They thought any important king would be born in a palace. But that wasn't God's plan. They asked King Herod, "Where is this king of the Jews who has been born? We've come to see Him."

Remember, Herod was the king. He didn't want there to be a new king. So he was mad. He told the wise men to find Jesus and bring Him back so Herod could worship Jesus too. But he was lying to the wise men. He really wanted to kill Jesus!

The men followed the star and found Jesus. They brought Him gifts of gold, frankincense, and myrrh—gifts fit for a king. God warned the wise men to go home a different way and not tell King Herod where Jesus was. Even though Herod was king and had a plan, God is the true King and had a bigger plan!

"Kira, do we give gifts at Christmas to remember the gifts brought to Jesus?"

"Yes, Bailey, we do!"

"I wish I could give Jesus a gift."

"You can! You can give Him the gift of following Him and loving Him."

HIDING GOD'S WORD IN YOUR HEART

What gift would you like to give to Jesus?

If you then, who are evil, know how to give good gifts to your children, how much more will your Father who is in heaven give good things to those who ask him! (Matthew 7:11)

John Baptizes Jesus

Matthew 3

"Watch out, Jacob!"

"Aahhh, I'm soaked, Olivia!"

"Ha-ha! Remember when Pastor Smith baptized Owen with water last week?"

"Yeah—but you're wearing a swimsuit. He had to do it in his clothes!"

"Why do we get baptized, Mom?"

"Well, it's a public sign that we're followers of Christ. Even Jesus was baptized. I'll tell you about it."

🌿 LET'S LEARN FROM GOD'S WORD

John the Baptist was an *unusual* man. He lived away from town, out in the wilderness—and he looked like it. He wore animal skins for clothes and ate honey straight from the beehive. He even ate bugs! People thought he wasn't "normal." But sometimes not being "normal" is a good thing.

See, God had a big plan for John the Baptist. It was his job to tell the people of Israel that the kingdom of God was coming, and it was coming soon.

"Prepare the way of the Lord," he said. "Repent from your sins and be baptized."

Even though John was different, people listened to him. They lined up to be baptized in the Jordan River. John baptized them with the same water that had

given life to the people of Israel for a long, long time. He said, "This water is a sign of your repentance, but One who is much greater than I am is coming soon."

Then, one day, He was there. The One who was greater, Jesus Christ. He stood near the bank of the Jordan River, and He asked John to baptize Him. "No," John said. "It is You who must baptize me!"

But, of course, John did as Jesus asked. He baptized Jesus, and the heavens opened. The Spirit of God came down like a pure white dove. And a voice spoke: "This is My beloved Son, with whom I am well pleased."

"Why don't we get baptized in rivers, Mom?"

"Some people do, Jacob. Some churches sprinkle water on people's foreheads, others dunk them in a tub, and others go out to the river and do it there. But for all Christians, baptism is a sign that we've been washed by God."

"And is God pleased by this, like He was with Jesus?"

"Yes, Olivia. He is!"

HIDING GOD'S WORD IN YOUR HEART

Have you ever seen a baptism? What happened?

Repent and be baptized every one of you in the name of Jesus Christ for the forgiveness of your sins, and you will receive the gift of the Holy Spirit. (Acts 2:38)

Satan Tempts Jesus in the Desert
Matthew 4:1–11

"Grandma, it's show-and-tell at school tomorrow. May I take Grandpa's baseball?"

"No, dear. Grandpa's not here to ask, and that ball has been his pride and joy for a long time. If anything happened to it, I believe you'd feel just terrible."

Ugh, I already promised my friends I'd bring Grandpa's ball. Maybe I should just take it and then put it right back where it was. He and Grandma would never even know ...

LET'S LEARN FROM GOD'S WORD

It's hard to say no when you really, really want to do something but know you shouldn't. That's called being *tempted*. Did you know even Jesus was tempted while He was on earth?

Jesus had gone up into the wilderness to pray and spend time with God. He fasted for forty days and forty nights. That means He didn't have *any* food during that time! He got hungry. Worst of all, Satan was tempting Him.

First, Satan tried to tempt Jesus to eat. But Jesus knew exactly what to do. He answered with a Bible verse: "Man doesn't live by bread alone, but by the word of God."

Then Satan took Jesus over to a high cliff. He told Jesus to throw Himself over the cliff and let angels protect Him. But Jesus had another Bible verse ready: "You shouldn't test God."

Finally, Satan told Jesus that he'd give Him all the kingdoms of the world and all the fame Jesus wanted if only Jesus would worship Satan. But Jesus knew that wasn't God's plan. So Jesus said, "The Bible tells us to worship only God."

That's when Satan gave up. Jesus knew the Bible. And He knew the Bible is always the best weapon against temptation.

"I guess you're right. The Bible tells me to honor my parents and grandparents. I can find something else that's cool—like this baseball card Grandpa gave me. My friends will like that too."

"Good idea, my dear grandson. And maybe Grandpa can pick you up from school and bring his baseball with him!"

HIDING GOD'S WORD IN YOUR HEART

What is your best weapon to fight against temptation?

Jesus said to him, "Be gone, Satan! For it is written,
'You shall worship the Lord your God
and him only shall you serve.'" (Matthew 4:10)

Jesus Chooses Twelve Disciples

Matthew 4:18–22; 10

"Don't forget, class, next week is our big service project! We're going to be collecting blankets and food to take to our neighbors downtown who don't have homes this winter. I'm going to need some volunteers to help me get everything organized. You'll be my helpers."

"Like Jesus's disciples!"

"That's a good comparison, Olivia. The disciples learned how to share Jesus's message of hope and forgiveness with the rest of the world. And when you help care for the poor downtown, you're bringing them hope too. So, who wants to help?"

🌿 LET'S LEARN FROM GOD'S WORD

Jesus had been here on earth for about thirty years. He had studied Scripture and learned to be a carpenter, like His dad.

When He came back out of the desert after being tempted by Satan, it was time for Jesus to begin sharing the good news with the world. But first He would need a team of people. These people would be His closest friends, His helpers in His ministry. And they would continue to tell the good news after Jesus was gone because He wasn't going to be on the earth for very long.

Did Jesus pick the people everyone expected: the teachers at the temple or the leaders in the town? Not exactly. God's plan is usually different from what we expect. Jesus listened for His voice.

Him, God whispered. And Jesus called the thunderous, rambunctious fishermen.

Him, God whispered again. And Jesus called the tax collector.

Him, God said. And Jesus called the financial expert who would one day break Jesus's heart.

These twelve men were the disciples of Jesus, and they walked with Him wherever He went. They were with Jesus every day for three years. Jesus healed the sick, raised the dead, cleansed the leapers, and cast out demons—all in the name of God the Father. After Jesus was gone, the disciples would continue to spread the good news of Jesus all over the world because they had seen it and they also knew it was true.

"Dad! As part of our missions project, we're going to spread God's love downtown by taking people blankets and food."

"Oh, wow! That sounds great, kids!"

"I can't wait! We're going to be like Jesus's disciples and spread the good news of God to everyone."

HIDING GOD'S WORD IN YOUR HEART

How do you think God may want you to help do His work?

I heard the voice of the Lord saying, "Whom shall I send, and who will go for us?" Then I said, "Here I am! Send me." (Isaiah 6:8)

The Dead Girl Is Alive Again

Luke 8:40–42, 49–56

"Thanks for coming to the hospital, Kira. I'm so glad you came. The doctor has been using a lot of big words, and my mom was crying. Her friend Monica is really sick."

"Bailey, what about you? Are you doing okay?"

"Yes. Well, no. I'm actually a little bit scared."

"I understand. But you know what? I trust God to take care of our friend. Let me tell you the story of the sick little girl in the Bible."

LET'S LEARN FROM GOD'S WORD

By now Jesus had become quite famous. He'd been healing the sick and telling people about God's love. When He went into towns, big crowds waited to meet Jesus. Everyone wanted a chance to touch Him and hear His voice, especially the people who were really sad or hurting.

One man who felt this way was Jairus. He was an important man in town, a leader at the synagogue. Leaders at the synagogue didn't usually run to Jesus to ask for help. But Jairus's daughter was very, very sick. So he came to Jesus because he needed help. He needed hope.

As soon as He heard Jairus's story, Jesus headed toward his house. But other people along the way wanted His help too. As they slowly moved down the street, Jairus saw one of his servants. "Don't bother Jesus," the servant said. "Your daughter has died."

Can you imagine how sad Jairus felt? Maybe he fell to the ground and cried. He loved his daughter very, very much!

But Jesus told him, "Don't be afraid. Your daughter is only sleeping."

Then Jesus went with Jairus to his house. Jesus took the sick girl's hand. "Wake up, child," He said. And just like that, she woke up.

They gave her some food and Jesus said, "Let's keep this one a secret, okay?" Jairus and his wife were amazed and they worshipped God. It was a day they would never, ever forget. That was probably a very hard secret for them to keep. What do you think?

"Bailey, Kira, good news! Monica is awake. Come see her. She wants you to pray with her."

"Praise God from whom all blessings flow!"

HIDING GOD'S WORD IN YOUR HEART

What can you praise God for today?

Bless the LORD, O my soul,
    and all that is within me,
      bless his holy name! (Psalm 103:1)

The Lord's Prayer

Matthew 6:9–13

"Emma, it's lunchtime!"

"I'm so hungry, Mom. Juice, sandwiches ... and grapes! I just love grapes!"

"Before we start to eat, don't forget to pray, Emma.

"Let's practice the Lord's Prayer. It goes like this ..."

LET'S LEARN FROM GOD'S WORD

Our Father in heaven,

Even though God lives in heaven, He loves us like a daddy would.

Hallowed be your name.

His name is perfect and holy. We must always respect it.

Your kingdom come,

One day everything will be right in the world.

Your will be done,

And everyone will follow God's plan.

On earth as it is in heaven.

But we can do our best to make life here look like life in heaven.

Give us this day our daily bread,

God alone can provide the things we need.

And forgive us our debts,

And God alone can forgive us when we sin.

As we also have forgiven our debtors.

But we'll do our best to forgive those people who hurt us too.

And lead us not into temptation,

God helps us make good choices.

But deliver us from evil.

And God encourages us so that we don't sin.

"Mom, is this the prayer that Jesus taught His disciples?"

"Yes, that's right. And not just the disciples, but everyone."

"Can we say the Lord's Prayer together when we eat lunch, Mom?"

"Yes, let's plan to do that every Sunday when we have our favorite foods."

HIDING GOD'S WORD IN YOUR HEART

Can you say the Lord's Prayer? Try putting hand motions to each line, to help you remember.

Pray in the Spirit on all occasions with all kinds of prayers and requests. With this in mind, be alert and always keep on praying for all the Lord's people. (Ephesians 6:18 NIV)

Jesus Feeds Five Thousand People
Matthew 14:13–21

"Have a great day at school, Emma!"

"Bye, Mom!" *Oh no! I don't see my lunch bag! And Mom packed my favorite snack. What am I going to do? I really don't want to be hungry! God, will You please help me?*

LET'S LEARN FROM GOD'S WORD

Jesus had had a long, hard week. And He'd just gotten really bad news—His cousin John the Baptist had died. Jesus just wanted to spend some time alone talking with God.

But the people wanted to be around Jesus so badly and hear what He had to say, so they followed Him. And what do you think He did?

Of course, Jesus helped them.

Even though His heart was sad, Jesus wanted to make other hearts happy. So when they brought people who were so sick that doctors weren't able to help them, Jesus made them better. Can you imagine how happy they must have felt?

It started to get late, and the disciples hadn't brought dinner with them. They were way out in the country. The disciples were going to tell the people to head home so they could all get dinner.

But Jesus told them to wait. He had a better plan. (He usually does.)

A boy offered to share his lunch of two fish and five loaves of bread. That wasn't very much food, especially for such a big crowd of people! But Jesus blessed the food for God's glory and asked the disciples to pass it out to everyone. It was amazing: every time Jesus broke off another piece, there was more to share!

More than five thousand people ate dinner with Jesus that night, and twelve baskets of extra food were left! Jesus saw what the people needed and He helped them. Then, when everyone left, He went back up the mountain by Himself so He could pray.

"Emma, great news! The school secretary just told me your mom dropped off your lunch bag. Do you want to pick a partner to walk with you to the office to get it?"

"Yes, thank you, Mrs. Jones!" *Thank You, God, for hearing my prayer for help. I was so hungry!*

HIDING GOD'S WORD IN YOUR HEART

What is your prayer to God today?

Do not be anxious about your life, what you will eat or what you will drink, nor about your body, what you will put on. Is not life more than food, and the body more than clothing? (Matthew 6:25)

Do Not Worry

Matthew 6:25–34

"Bailey, what's wrong?"

"I'm scared to go to sleep. I've been having nightmares."

"Oh, sweetie, that's hard. I'm so sorry. Would you like me to pray with you, and then maybe I can tell you a story that will give you a good dream instead?"

"Yes, that would be great. Thanks!"

LET'S LEARN FROM GOD'S WORD

King David—you remember him, right? He was the shepherd boy who wrote so many psalms, killed Goliath with a slingshot, and grew into a man after God's own heart (even though he made some pretty huge mistakes too). And David had a son named Solomon.

Remember Solomon? He was very wise and very, very rich. He had a beautiful palace and the most amazing food and drinks, and people (even kings and queens from other nations) traveled very far just to visit him and see his over-the-top lifestyle. It's easy to say most people in the world would have loved to live just like Solomon.

But do you know what Jesus said? Even Solomon, in all his splendor, wasn't dressed any more beautifully than flowers in the fields, or even at the park. God takes care of them, and He'll take care of you too.

"Bailey, God loves you so much. If He made the flowers to be so beautiful, more beautiful than a king, then He values you too. He is watching out for you, even when you're asleep. Do you believe that?"

"I do! I'm going to try to sleep now, but will you come check on me in a little while? I know God's watching, but it makes me feel better to know you are too."

"Of course. Good night!"

HIDING GOD'S WORD IN YOUR HEART

Have you seen a beautiful flower? How are you like that flower in God's eyes?

But seek first his kingdom and his righteousness, and all these things will be given to you as well. Therefore do not worry about tomorrow, for tomorrow will worry about itself. (Matthew 6:33–34 NIV)

The Good Helper

Luke 10:25–37

"Jacob, did you see that new kid at lunch today, sitting by himself?"

"Yes, and then some boys from our class started picking on him."

"I feel bad that I didn't stop them. But I was in a hurry. And they're such horrible bullies, I was afraid."

"Kids, there's a story from the Bible that might help you know what to do …"

LET'S LEARN FROM GOD'S WORD

In Israel there were two kinds of people—the Samaritans and everyone else. Well, not really. There were a lot more kinds of people than that. But all the Jews thought the Samaritans were horrible people to be avoided (which isn't very nice at all, is it?).

Once when Jesus was teaching, He said that we should love our neighbors. Then someone asked Jesus who our neighbors really are. He told them a story that made them rethink how they viewed the Samaritans. This was the story He told:

Once a man—probably an upstanding Jewish man—was walking from Jerusalem to Jericho. This was a very dangerous journey. Sure enough, the man was attacked by robbers and left alone—very hurt, very scared, and very much in need of a friend.

A priest happened to be coming by, so surely he helped the man, right? No, he hurried on his way, passing over to the other side of the road. Next a Levite came along. Levites helped out at God's house, what we know as church today. Surely this man would help? Nope, he just kept on walking. Finally a Samaritan came along the road. And, he helped the man! He cared for his wounds and helped him get to a hotel safely, and he also gave the hotel owner money to take care of anything the man would need to get well again.

Then Jesus asked the crowd, "Who was being a good neighbor?" And they knew the answer—it wasn't the two people who were like the man who was robbed but the Samaritan who, although he was very different from him, showed him mercy. Then Jesus said to go and show mercy too.

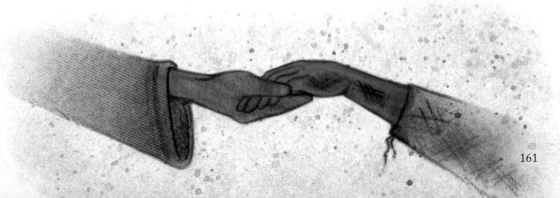

"Kids, it sounds like you both missed a chance to help out the new kid at school."

"Actually, Dad, I did stop to help. I found out his name is Robert. He seems like a decent guy."

"Jacob, I'm proud of you. Way to go."

"Dad, maybe we could ask him over on Saturday. Then I can get to know him too."

"Good idea, Olivia.

HIDING GOD'S WORD IN YOUR HEART

When did you want to help someone, but didn't? What happened?

We must help the weak, remembering the words the Lord Jesus himself said: "It is more blessed to give than to receive."

(Acts 20:35 NIV)

Zacchaeus: The Man Who Wanted to See God

Luke 19:1–10

"Grandpa, what kind of tree is this one? It's so tall!"

"That's a sycamore, Jackson. It's a great tree, but you'll have to climb it next time around. Your mom and dad are waiting for you. It's time to head home."

"Aw, I'm not ready to go yet."

"How about this? You hop down out of that tree and while we're heading to the car, I'll tell you a story about a man in the Bible who climbed a tree!"

LET'S LEARN FROM GOD'S WORD

Zacchaeus was a tax collector for the Roman government. Tax collectors took money from the Jews to send back to Rome. They weren't exactly the most popular people in town.

Zacchaeus had heard that this man Jesus wasn't just healing the sick and doing miracles but was also being kind to tax collectors, something most people weren't. So Zacchaeus decided to go and see what the talk was all about.

But Zacchaeus was very short. As the crowd waiting for Jesus grew bigger, Zacchaeus couldn't see. So he climbed up in a tree. That wasn't something a lot of grown-ups did, but he really wanted to see Jesus when He walked by.

Zacchaeus had no idea Jesus would be able to see *him* so clearly! Jesus looked at him and said, "Zacchaeus, come down. Let's go have dinner at your house."

Me? Zacchaeus thought. *He's talking to me?*

The others wondered the same thing. Why in the world would Jesus eat at the house of a sinner like Zacchaeus, someone who cheated people out of their money? But God had a plan—a plan to change Zacchaeus's heart.

When Zacchaeus felt Jesus's love and compassion, he wanted to love others too. He decided he'd give half of everything he owned to the poor. Wow, that's a lot! He also said that he would give back the money he stole from people—four times as much as what he took.

Zacchaeus was a sinner and had made some mistakes, but God forgave him. So Zacchaeus wanted to spend the rest of his life giving to others.

"Are you ready to head home now, Jackson?"

"Yes. I'm sorry I didn't get out of that tree right away, Mom and Dad. Grandpa, do you promise I can climb that tree again next time I come over?"

"Of course, Jackson. I can't wait."

"Me either! I'm going to think about it all the way home."

"Ha-ha! Good idea, young man. See you soon!"

HIDING GOD'S WORD IN YOUR HEART

♥

When did you make the wrong decision the first time around? What happened?

The Son of Man came to seek and to save the lost. (Luke 19:10)

Hosanna! Jesus's Triumphal Entry

John 12:12–19

"I love Palm Sunday! That means Easter is almost here. My favorite part is waving these palm branches. And I love shouting 'Hosanna!' Do you know that means 'save us!'? Our pastor will tell you the story."

LET'S LEARN FROM GOD'S WORD

It was time for Passover in Jerusalem. Passover was a huge festival. People traveled to Jerusalem from all over. They had feasts and celebrations to remember God rescuing them out of slavery in Egypt. (Do you remember the story of Moses leading the people out of Egypt? That was the first Passover. People were still celebrating hundreds of years later!)

But there was something extra special about this Passover: Jesus was coming to Jerusalem!

As Jesus did miracles and cast out demons and raised people from the dead, the people started to realize He was someone very special. He was more than just

a man. They started to believe He was the Messiah. The One the prophets had talked about so long ago. The One they'd been waiting for!

As Jesus entered the city, riding on a donkey, people shouted, "Hosanna!" (You know what this means now.) And they waved palm branches and laid their coats down in front of Jesus as a way to show honor. You see, they thought Jesus was going to be the new king of Israel. They hoped Jesus would save them from the Roman rulers.

Of course, as you know by now, God's plans are usually different from people's plans. Jesus wouldn't be a king in the world. He would be a much better King of kings, a heavenly King, as we will find out.

"Emma, you did great! Let's take your palm branch home with us."

"Mom, what is Passion Week?"

"Oh, that is the last week of Jesus's life before He died on the cross so we could be forgiven of our sins. Palm Sunday starts Passion Week."

"Hosanna! Hosanna in the highest!"

HIDING GOD'S WORD IN YOUR HEART

♥

Do you remember what "hosanna" means? What does it mean that Jesus saves us?

> Who is this King of glory?
> The LORD of hosts,
> he is the King of glory! (Psalm 24:10)

The Last Supper
Luke 22:7–20

"Kira, I'm starving! Look at all this food!"

"I know. We have great cooks in the family! Hey, Uncle Joe is getting us started."

"Come on around, everybody. Let's hold hands while we pray before this amazing lunch. You know, I'm so happy we can all be together for Easter. Before we enjoy this meal God has provided for us, let's talk a little bit about the last meal Jesus had with His disciples. Then we can celebrate our faith while we eat."

✎ LET'S LEARN FROM GOD'S WORD

Jesus and His disciples had traveled to Jerusalem. They needed to find a place to have their Passover meal. So Jesus sent Peter and John into the city. "When you have just gotten inside the city gates," Jesus told them, "you'll find a man carrying a jar of water. Tell his master that the Teacher wants to use his extra room to celebrate Passover with the disciples."

Sure enough, it happened just as Jesus said. The disciples found the man with the water. His master had a room where they could eat the Passover meal together. That night the disciples gathered there with Jesus. They passed the Passover lamb

around the table to the real Passover Lamb (yes, it was Jesus) who would become the ultimate, final sacrifice just a couple of days later.

They passed the wine and the bread made without yeast (just like on the night of the first Passover). They all shared it together.

As they ate, Jesus spoke to them. He said that every time they ate or drank that meal, they were to remember Him. Does this remind you of something we eat and drink at church? Yes, it's like Communion! When we eat the bread and drink the wine (or juice) together at church, we show the people around us that we're committed to remembering Jesus's sacrifice.

"Uncle Joe, I take Communion at church too! It's not just snack time—it's really important. It's the way we show everyone we love God. When we share in His Communion meal, we're saying we're part of His family."

"That's right, Bailey! Communion is a wonderful time to pray and thank Jesus for His sacrifice and for allowing us to be part of His family forever."

HIDING GOD'S WORD IN YOUR HEART

What happens at church when you celebrate the Lord's Supper?

He took bread, and when he had given thanks, he broke it and gave it to them, saying, "This is my body, which is given for you. Do this in remembrance of me." (Luke 22:19)

Prayers in the Garden

Matthew 26:36–46

"Mom, I feel like no matter what I'm doing—whether I'm happy or worried or frustrated or scared—the Lord's Prayer makes me feel like God loves me and everything is going to be okay."

"Yes, Emma. Prayer is so important. No matter where you are or what's going on, you can always talk to God. You know, Jesus prayed too."

"You mean He prayed more than the Lord's Prayer? Did Jesus ever get scared?"

"Well, the night before He was going to die, He went to a garden to spend time praying to God. Let's take a look and see what happened."

LET'S LEARN FROM GOD'S WORD

One of Jesus's disciples, Judas, left the Passover dinner earlier than the rest of the disciples. He was going to meet the religious leaders—the ones who didn't like Jesus—to tell them where they could find Jesus. They wanted to put Jesus on trial and punish Him for the things He was doing and saying.

Jesus knew what was happening. He knew God required a perfect, holy sacrifice to take away the sins of His people. And He knew that God's plan, all along, was for His very own Son, Jesus, to be that perfect sacrifice.

But it wasn't going to be easy.

Jesus asked the disciples to go to a garden with Him to pray. It was late at night, and they'd just eaten a big meal. Instead of staying awake with their friend Jesus, who was really having a hard time, they fell asleep.

Meanwhile, Jesus was talking to God. "Is it possible there could be another plan, Father? Could We do this another way? But I know it's Your plan, not Mine, that must happen. I am willing to follow You."

Jesus went to His disciples and woke them up. He said, "Friends, this is a very hard time for me. Please stay awake and be praying for me." He also knew the next day would be very hard for His disciples too, so it would be good for them to spend time in prayer.

But you know what happened? As soon as Jesus went back to talk to God, the disciples fell asleep again. How do you think that made Jesus feel?

"Mom, I bet Jesus wished He could talk to His Dad in person that night. Sometimes I wish I could talk to my heavenly Daddy in person too."

"I know, sweetie. I do too. But God is always with us and we can talk to Him in prayer whenever we want to. Even though we can't see Him, He's listening. One day we will be able to see Him in heaven. It's going to be wonderful. And it's possible only because of what Jesus did."

HIDING GOD'S WORD IN YOUR HEART

Have you prayed to God, asking for help doing something you didn't want to do? When?

Pray without ceasing. (1 Thessalonians 5:17)

Peter: The Man Who Loved but Denied Jesus

Mark 14:27–31; Luke 22:54–62

"Hey, Olivia! Are you coming to Ava's party this weekend?"

"Yes, I can't wait."

"Oh my goodness, you guys. Look over there at Addie. How embarrassing! Why is she doing that?"

"Wait. Isn't she your friend, Olivia?"

"What? No. I mean, she sat at my table at lunch, but she's not my friend."

"Yeah, she's so weird. See you at the party!"

🖋 LET'S LEARN FROM GOD'S WORD

Jesus had been in the garden praying for a while when He and the disciples saw Roman soldiers and Jewish servants coming to arrest Him. At the front of the pack was one of Jesus's own disciples, Judas.

Judas walked forward and kissed Jesus on the cheek. It was a sign of friendship, but Judas used it to show the enemy which man was Jesus. The guards tried to grab Jesus, and Jesus allowed Himself to be arrested because He knew it was God's plan.

One of Jesus's disciples, Peter, followed as the guards took Jesus to the high priest's home. He sat with some servants in the courtyard, warming himself by the fire.

A servant girl asked him, "Aren't you one of Jesus's friends?"

Right away, Peter said no. The servant girl didn't believe him. She started telling others that Peter was a friend of Jesus. Peter said no again. A little later, someone else asked Peter if he knew Jesus. Peter said no a third time. Have you ever said something you wish you could take back? That's how Peter felt. He remembered that Jesus had told him the night before that this would happen. He felt so bad that he started crying.

The exciting thing about this story is that a few days later Jesus rose from the dead and forgave Peter! Jesus asked Peter three times if he loved Him. And Peter said three times, "I love You!" But we're getting ahead of ourselves. Before we can celebrate Jesus coming back to life, we need to understand how His death was part of God's plan too.

"Hey, Addie! Can I help?"

"Sure, Olivia. That's nice of you."

"No problem. Hey, I was wondering if you might want to come over this weekend to my house. If you can put up with my twin brother, Jacob!"

HIDING GOD'S WORD IN YOUR HEART

Have you ever pretended you weren't friends with someone, even though you were?

[Peter] said, "Lord, you know everything. You know that I love you." Jesus said, "Then feed my sheep." (John 21:17 NLT)

Jesus's Death
Luke 23

"Kira, I was thinking about today being Good Friday. It kind of fits that it's raining today, doesn't it?"

"Yeah, Bailey. Good Friday is a sad day. It's a wonderful day, but a sad one."

"I wish there had been some other way we could have been forgiven of our sins, so Jesus wouldn't have had to die."

"Me too. But I'm so, so thankful Jesus was obedient to God's plan. Without His obedience, we would have no hope of a future with God. And that's a really sad thought."

🖋 LET'S LEARN FROM GOD'S WORD

Jesus had been declared guilty. Of course, He was guilty of nothing. In fact, He is the only person who's never done anything wrong. But Pilate, the governor, declared Him guilty anyway. Jesus would have to die.

The Roman soldiers took Jesus's clothes and placed a crown of thorns on His head. The crown was a way to make fun of Him, since people believed Jesus was the king of the Jews. They whipped Him so badly that His back bled, and they made Him carry a huge wooden cross. It was the cross they would hang Him from up on top of a hill.

When Jesus couldn't carry it any longer, the soldiers grabbed a man named Simon from the crowd and made him carry it. I wonder what Simon was thinking as he walked. Did he stay while they nailed Jesus's hands to the cross?

Two other people were killed on crosses that day—two criminals. Jesus wasn't a criminal. But He knew God had a plan, and He knew that plan was good. So He was faithful. Because Jesus died on the cross, we can receive forgiveness and the chance to be part of God's family.

"Bailey, let's see if anyone else is up yet. Maybe we can make some pancakes for breakfast."

"That sounds really good."

"And you know what we can look forward to? Easter! Jesus is risen! I can't wait to celebrate on Sunday."

HIDING GOD'S WORD IN YOUR HEART

What do you do to remember Good Friday? And how do you celebrate Easter?

There is therefore now no condemnation for those who are in Christ Jesus. For the law of the Spirit of life has set you free in Christ Jesus from the law of sin and death. (Romans 8:1–2)

Jesus Is Risen!

Matthew 28:1–10; Mark 16; Luke 24; John 20

"Happy Easter, Jackson!"

"Happy Easter, Grandpa! What are you doing?"

"Well, I was just reading about that first Easter morning, and I was wondering what it was like when Jesus's friends realized He had risen from the dead."

"I bet they were so excited. And maybe a little confused. What do you think?"

"Well, let's take a look and see.

🖋 LET'S LEARN FROM GOD'S WORD

Two women, both named Mary, got up really, really early that morning. The sun was just beginning to rise. They were very sad because their friend Jesus had died. They wanted to go to His tomb and put spices on His body.

When they got to the place, the ground started shaking! An angel of the Lord came down from heaven and rolled away the stone in front of Jesus's tomb. His face was so bright it shone like lightning!

"Don't be afraid," the angel told the women. "I know you're looking for your friend, Jesus. I have awesome news: He's alive! Let me show you!"

What do you think the women thought when they saw the empty tomb? I wonder if they were so surprised they couldn't even talk. Maybe that's why the

Bible doesn't tell us anything about what they said. Instead, the angel told them (perhaps with a happy laugh), "Go, tell the disciples. You'll see Jesus in Galilee. Go, now! Hurry! It's great news!"

The women were terrified but also very happy as they ran all the way back to the disciples. As they went, do you know who they saw? Jesus! Their beloved friend Jesus was alive.

The women fell at Jesus's feet and worshipped Him. "Don't be afraid," Jesus told them. "Go tell the others that I will see them soon too!"

The news was too good not to share. You and I get to share the good news too because it's really, really great news!

"Good morning, gentlemen! What has you both up so early?"

"It's Easter, Grandma! Jesus is alive!"

"Yes, He is. He's alive. Alleluia!"

"When I hear the Easter story, I remember that I didn't do anything to deserve to be in God's family. But I get to be because of Jesus!"

"Yes, Jackson. We call it the gift of grace. And it's a wonderful thing."

HIDING GOD'S WORD IN YOUR HEART

Why is it such good news that Jesus rose from the dead?

God, being rich in mercy, because of the great love with which he loved us, even when we were dead in our trespasses, made us alive together with Christ—by grace you have been saved. (Ephesians 2:4–5)

Telling the World the Good News

Matthew 28:16–20

"Kira, Darek! I won! I won, I won, I won!"

"What did you win?"

"Mrs. Graham had a contest at school. Everyone's name was in the pot, and she was giving away a scooter. She pulled my name! I won! I got a brand-new scooter. It's soooo awesome!"

"Wow, Bailey! Do you want to go out and play with it? Be sure to share with your friends out there too."

"I will. I'm so excited, I can't wait to tell everyone."

"You know, that reminds me of something Jesus told His disciples ..."

LET'S LEARN FROM GOD'S WORD

The disciples were so excited. Jesus, their Savior, was alive again! They couldn't believe it. They wanted to spend all their time with Him. But that time would be short, Jesus said. Soon He would be going back to heaven to be with His Father. He'd always be watching them, though. And He would also send His Holy Spirit to be with them here on earth.

The disciples had a new job. God wanted them to share the excitement they were feeling! Not just with their families or their neighbors. Not just with their towns and the people nearby. They needed to share it with the whole world—with people from every country!

That would take a really long time, right? Those twelve disciples couldn't do it all on their own. The Holy Spirit was helping them, and other people were joining them. In fact, the job to pass on excitement about Jesus is given to everyone who believes in Him—including us!

It's great, awesome, amazing news. Even better news than winning a new scooter. Because when that scooter is old and rusty or you've gotten too old for it, your salvation from Jesus will still be a gift that's more precious than anything else.
It will never, ever fade.

"You know what, I'm going to go out and play. And I'm going to tell my friends about my new scooter ... and about how much Jesus loves us. That's two pieces of good news!"

"Yes, it sure is, Bailey! Wear your helmet and have fun."

HIDING GOD'S WORD IN YOUR HEART

Have you told anyone about Jesus's love? Will you tell others that He died for them and He forgives them of their sins?

Go therefore and make disciples of all nations, baptizing them in the name of the Father and of the Son and of the Holy Spirit, teaching them to observe all that I have commanded you. And behold, I am with you always, to the end of the age. (Matthew 28:19–20)

The Holy Spirit Lives with God's People

Acts 1–2

"Ooh, Grandpa. I really don't like that wind."

"I know—it's really powerful, isn't it, Jackson? But it reminds me of something."

"What?"

"Have you ever heard the story of Pentecost?"

"Penta-what?"

"Ha-ha! Let me tell you about it …"

✒ LET'S LEARN FROM GOD'S WORD

Jesus had met with His disciples after He rose from the dead and told them that it was time for Him to go back up to heaven to be with His Father. They'd see Him again, but not here on earth. In the meantime, He was sending a helper to come and be with them. This helper was called the Holy Spirit, and they'd know He was there even though He wasn't someone they could see with their eyes.

So they gathered together to celebrate the festival of Pentecost, just as they always did, when suddenly a very strong wind—probably the strongest they'd ever felt—came directly from heaven to earth and filled the room they were in.

196

Then something like a flame appeared, split apart into a lot of little flames, and came to stop over each of their heads. The disciples began to praise God. Even though people from many countries were at the festival and all spoke different languages, God made it so the people could understand in their own language what the disciples were saying. It was a miracle!

And this was the moment the Holy Spirit came to live among God's people, to be their helper and to help them understand the message of God's good news until Jesus comes again.

"So, maybe when I hear the loud wind, I should just remember that it's a sign of how strong God really is?"

"Yes, Jackson, I think that's a wonderful idea."

"I wish I had been there on that day. Hearing all those different languages and being able to understand them all. Wow! That would be amazing."

"It sure would. Now let's go feed those chickens. They sure are letting us know in their language that it's feeding time, with all their squabbling and squawking!"

HIDING GOD'S WORD IN YOUR HEART

♥

Do you have a friend who speaks a different language? Did you know that God knows how to speak all languages?

In the last days, God says,
    I will pour out my Spirit on all people....
And everyone who calls
    on the name of the Lord will be saved. (Acts 2:17, 21 NIV)

Starting the New Church

Acts 2:42–47

"Look at all these people in purple shirts, Kira. What are they doing?"

"Let's go ask. Hi there. We were wondering what you guys were doing?"

"We're from that church over there on the corner. We're having a vacation Bible school in a few weeks, and we'd love for you to come learn about Jesus."

"Cool! Kira, are they missionaries?"

"Yes, I think they are. If they're telling people about God, then that's living like a missionary."

LET'S LEARN FROM GOD'S WORD

More and more people heard about Jesus and believed in Him. Before long there were hundreds and then thousands of people who knew the good news. They needed to get organized so they could work together to spread the message to every country in the world, as Jesus asked them to do.

It was time to start a church.

The people who started meeting together as the first church of believers in Jesus Christ loved to get together to pray, listen to teaching about Jesus, and worship. They ate meals together. They even shared all their possessions so that everyone had the things they needed.

Every day more people came to believe in Jesus because God's followers were known as people who loved one another and took care of one another.

"So, how about it? Do you want to go to that vacation Bible school?"

"Well, I'm not sure, Kira. Darek, would you go if I go?"

"Yes, Bailey, I would. Just think, we could make some more friends in our neighborhood."

"Right, and with summer coming, we could have fun playing at the park with them too."

"Besides, you'd be learning more about Jesus. And that's always a good thing!"

"Kira, you're right. Let's plan to go!"

HIDING GOD'S WORD IN YOUR HEART

Do you go to a church? What's your favorite thing you do at church?

Just as the body is one and has many members, and all the members of the body, though many, are one body, so it is with Christ.

(1 Corinthians 12:12)

Shipwrecked!

Acts 27:13–44

"Okay, kids. Here's how you do it. Stand up really straight and try not to wobble. See how long you can make it before you fall!"

"I got it, I got it! Oh, wait, no—" *Splash!*

"Jacob! I'm soaked. Ha-ha! Let's try again."

"Look, Dad, we're doing it!"

"Yeah, we're a ship out on the ocean."

"Oh no, here comes a wave. Shipwreck!" *Splash!*

"Let's swim to shore and take a break. Two shipwrecks in one day is a lot to survive."

LET'S LEARN FROM GOD'S WORD

Paul was an apostle of Jesus. He visited many cities, telling people about Jesus. But the religious leaders who had arrested Jesus and had him killed were angry at Paul. They got Paul arrested and tried to convince the Romans that Paul was dangerous and deserved to be killed like Jesus. But Paul convinced the Romans to give him a fair trial far away.

So the Romans put Paul on a boat guarded by an officer named Julius. It was a very long journey. As they stopped along the way, Julius was kind to Paul and let him get off the boat to visit his friends. Later, Paul warned Julius that the weather had turned bad. It would be dangerous to keep sailing. But Julius didn't listen and they kept going.

Sure enough, a huge storm came. The ship was tossed around on the water like a bathtub toy. The sailors lost control. They were sure they were going to die.

Then an angel visited Paul in the night and told him, "Don't give up." The angel said that everyone on the ship would be safe but they would be shipwrecked on an island.

What do you think happened? They saw land. They sailed toward it as fast as they could, but they ran into the ground and the ship started to break into pieces. The soldiers wanted to kill the prisoners, including Paul, so they wouldn't escape. But Julius stopped them. Instead, he told everyone who could swim to jump overboard and head toward shore. The others were to grab a plank and float in as best they could.

Do you think they made it? Yes! Just like God's messenger said, every one of them made it to shore safely. And the Word of God began to spread farther and farther to new countries. In fact, Paul wrote many letters to God's people and all the new churches popping up everywhere!

"Do you guys need a water break?"

"Watch out, Mom! The sea is stormy. Aahhh! Shipwreck!"

"I'm so glad you're all safe. God is so powerful and so good!"

"Yes. Let's go again!"

HIDING GOD'S WORD IN YOUR HEART

How has God protected you when you faced danger?

Fear not, for I am with you;
   be not dismayed, for I am your God. (Isaiah 41:10)

The Armor of God

Ephesians 6:10–18

"That's so cool, Dad! What is it?"

"It's ancient armor. Jacob is a warrior for God. This is his belt of truth right here, and his sword of the Spirit. And here's his shield and his breastplate to protect his heart."

"Olivia, that looks great! Do you want to know what God's armor really looks like?"

"Yes! Tell us."

LET'S LEARN FROM GOD'S WORD

Did you know that if you believe in God and follow Him, then you're a soldier in His army? It may be hard to see our Enemy, the Devil, sometimes, but he is there—like when someone says something mean to you, or you get afraid when the lights go out at night.

But God's soldiers are strong and good and brave. Here's their secret: they wear God's armor. In the Bible, the apostle Paul tells us that when we wear this armor, it will be impossible for the Enemy to win a battle against us. We'll be like superheroes. Isn't that awesome?

Here's what the armor looks like:

The belt is God's truth. If we remember God's truth, we won't believe the Devil's lies.

The armor over our whole body is God's righteousness. We aren't perfect, but Jesus is. When Satan attacks us, we can remind him that we're covered by Jesus's sacrifice.

Our shoes are peace. We can live peacefully because we know God's good news.

The shield we hold up in front of us as we walk through life is faith. Through faith in God, we can do anything!

We protect our head—and our minds—with salvation (which means eternal life with God in heaven), remembering that nothing at all can ever take us out of God's hand.

And last, but not least, is our very sharp, very powerful sword, which is the Bible. If we know the Bible, we'll be able to beat any spiritual enemy that tries to attack us.

"Wait, don't move! I want to get a picture of my little warriors first!"

"Mom, we're not really warriors, you know."

"Sure you are! The Bible says all God's children are warriors for good. And we have His spiritual armor for protection. You can pray to put it on every day before you leave the house. You'll have all the weapons you need to be in God's army."

"Cool!"

HIDING GOD'S WORD IN YOUR HEART

What is your favorite piece of armor God has given you? Why?

May the LORD give strength to his people!
May the LORD bless his people with peace! (Psalm 29:11)

John: The Man Who Saw Heaven

Revelation 21

"Are the cookies ready yet, Mom?"

"I'm just checking them now, Emma. They smell heavenly, don't they?"

"What do you mean by 'heavenly'? Will we have cookies in heaven?"

"Oh, I sure hope so. Tell me about your painting, Emma."

"Well, I started out painting my favorite place—the swing down by the river. But now I think I might make it be a picture of heaven."

"I love that. It's beautiful."

"Mom, will you tell me what you think heaven will be like?"

LET'S LEARN FROM GOD'S WORD

People have had many different ideas about what heaven will be like. Some say it's up in the clouds, where little babies have wings and play harps. Others say it's going to be just like the garden of Eden but without sin.

Did you know there's a book in the Bible called Revelation that describes what heaven will be like after Jesus returns to earth to be the once-and-for-all King? A man named John wrote Revelation after seeing a vision of heaven. Here's how John described what he saw:

The new city of Jerusalem shines like a precious stone. There's a high wall around the city, with four sides like a square. The wall has twelve gates in it—three on each side. On each of those gates are the names of the twelve tribes of Israel. The wall is set on twelve foundation stones. Each of those stones have the names of the twelve disciples on them.

The city is made of gold so pure you can see through it like glass. The walls are made of expensive gems, and the gates are made of pearl. The best thing is that the gates to the city will never, ever be shut. There will no longer be any night. And there will be nothing dirty, sad, or broken ever in the city. People will come there to praise God, to enjoy Him, and to worship Him. And that, my friend, is God's plan for *us*!

"I think the cookies are ready now. Would you like one?"

"Yes, please! Can we hang up my picture first?"

"Of course. You know, someday we'll see heaven for ourselves. And the things we can only imagine—like these beautiful images from your picture—will be as real as these cookies right here in front of us now."

"I think that sounds really, really great."

"Yes, honey, it does."

HIDING GOD'S WORD IN YOUR HEART

What do you think heaven will be like?

He will wipe away every tear from their eyes, and death shall be no more, neither shall there be mourning, nor crying, nor pain anymore, for the former things have passed away. (Revelation 21:4)

The Beginning and the End
Revelation 1:4–8

"Mom, if God is big and good and perfect, why does He need us to glorify Him?"

"Well, I don't think He *needs* us to glorify Him, Emma. But when we understand that He is perfectly good and that He loves us, then we can't help but worship Him."

"So it's not so much that God needs our worship but that He really, really wants us to know Him?"

"I couldn't have said it better myself."

LET'S LEARN FROM GOD'S WORD

Did you know that when Jesus comes back to earth, He will show up in the clouds while trumpets sound? All people on earth will recognize that He's the one true King. They'll remember He created this world in the first place, He saved His people from slavery in Egypt, He made Israel a mighty kingdom, and then He came as a baby to save His people from their sin.

When people see Him, they'll decide whether they'll follow Him forever in His kingdom that will never end.

Those who choose to follow Jesus will get to live in heaven with Him as their King. He is the beginning and the end, the Alpha and Omega, the most powerful God. He is holy, and we will get to worship Him and enjoy Him face-to-face forever.

It's going to be amazing!

"How will you end this story, Emma? You can write down your ending here. Or you can draw a picture of what you think life will be like when we're in heaven with Jesus."

HIDING GOD'S WORD IN YOUR HEART

What about you? Will you follow Jesus like the other kids in this book?

I am the Alpha and the Omega, the beginning and the end. To the thirsty I will give from the spring of the water of life without payment. (Revelation 21:6)

God's Everlasting Love
John 3:16–17

"Hey, guys! Can we play with you too?"

"Sure, Bailey! We were just talking about our favorite things. Mine is climbing trees, and Logan's is swinging. What's your favorite thing?"

"Oh, that's easy! Know what I love most of all? God! Because He loves me!"

"What do you mean? I've never seen God. How do you know He loves you?"

✒ LET'S LEARN FROM GOD'S WORD

Thousands of years ago God created the world. You remember that story, right? His creation was good, and the people He put in the world were very good. God loved the world He'd created.

But then the people became selfish and decided they'd follow their own wishes instead of doing what God told them to do. So they had to leave their beautiful home with God in the garden of Eden and go wander about the earth instead. The world wasn't perfect anymore.

The people were sad for a long time. No matter how many times God reminded the people that He loved them, they forgot. They kept going back to their sinful ways. So eventually God put His plan in place. His own Son would come down to earth—not just as God visiting man but as a man Himself. He would live a perfect life and then choose to die as the perfect sacrifice that was required for the forgiveness of sin. His name was Jesus.

When Jesus died He told His Father, "It is finished." This was the final sacrifice that covers all sins for all time. And anyone who is faithful to love God will get to live with Him forever.

That means you too! God loves you, and He wants you to live as His child. He wants you to enjoy Him and glorify Him with your life. He wants you to enjoy an abundant life with Him forever. Will you love Him too?

"Wow, Bailey! I never knew all that stuff about Jesus."

"Yeah, it's pretty amazing, isn't it, Brent?"

"Hey, I want to know more about this."

"Okay, Morgan! Well, you are all invited to come to my church. It's pretty fun, and it's just down the street. Right, Kira?"

"Yes, Bailey. We could all meet here at the park and walk over together if you want!"

HIDING GOD'S WORD IN YOUR HEART

♥

What do you think it means to live as God's child?

For God so loved the world, that he gave his only Son, that whoever believes in him should not perish but have eternal life. For God did not send his Son into the world to condemn the world, but in order that the world might be saved through him. (John 3:16–17)